BRIGHTER THAN SCALE, SWIFTER THAN FLAME

ALSO BY NEON YANG

THE TENSORATE SERIES
The Black Tides of Heaven
The Red Threads of Fortune
The Descent of Monsters
The Ascent to Godhood

The Genesis of Misery

BRIGHTER THAN SCALE, SWIFTER THAN FLAME

NEON YANG

Tor Publishing Group
New York

This is a work of fiction. All of the characters, organizations, and events portrayed in this novella are either products of the author's imagination or are used fictitiously.

BRIGHTER THAN SCALE, SWIFTER THAN FLAME

Copyright © 2025 by Neon Yang

All rights reserved.

A Tordotcom Book
Published by Tom Doherty Associates / Tor Publishing Group
120 Broadway
New York, NY 10271

www.torpublishinggroup.com

Tor® is a registered trademark of Macmillan Publishing Group, LLC.

The Library of Congress Cataloging-in-Publication Data is available upon request.

ISBN 978-1-250-35734-2 (hardcover)
ISBN 978-1-250-35735-9 (ebook)

Our books may be purchased in bulk for promotional, educational, or business use. Please contact your local bookseller or the Macmillan Corporate and Premium Sales Department at 1-800-221-7945, extension 5442, or by email at MacmillanSpecialMarkets@macmillan.com.

First Edition: 2025

Printed in the United States of America

0 9 8 7 6 5 4 3 2 1

*To my queer family. You are loved;
they cannot take love from us.*

BRIGHTER THAN SCALE, SWIFTER THAN FLAME

CHAPTER ONE

MANY TALES ARE told of the masked guildknight of Mithrandon. Tales as grand as the mountains and lofty as the moon, tales of conquest and triumph over evil. Heroic tales of dragon-slaying, where a fire-breathing fiend the size of a castle, a burner of fields and villages, is taken down by a single guildknight carrying the banner of the Sun Empire. The glacial wyrm over Studhern, who set a months-long winter over the town, freezing children in their beds: the masked guildknight cut its head off with one blow of their sacred weapon Varuhelt. The scourge of Callenden, who emptied the pastures of sheep and turned to cribs by the hearth instead: the masked guildknight chased it down with their wyrmhound Sage and tore it to ribbons in its lair, before smashing the five hundred eggs it had laid, five hundred beastly whelps that would have gone on to terrorize countless subjects of the Sun Empire. Elandis of Shereton sings of the knight's first conquest, a wyrm they vanquished as a mere child of five, cutting it in half as the beast stood on some rocky outcrop by the fields of the mystical village in which they grew up. Whether or not such a place exists is not important. The guildknight's triumph: that is the real story. Picture them parading through some city they have just saved, its streets frothing with joy like a brook after the spring rains. Imagine the glorious sunbeams leaping off their helmet and unblemished armor, giving their form a perfect and pleasing silhouette. Drums are beat and petals tossed into the air in ebullient bursts of color. Their winged carriage is white and peerless, pulled by their fearsome gryphons Carys and Meteor with their high arched necks and glossy flanks. A painter's canvas would be elevated by the depiction of such a glorious scene.

Yet for all that is told about the guildknight of Mithrandon, what do we truly know of them? In all of these stories nothing is said of the person who they were: not their name, their age, nor where they came from. Who they were raised by and who they loved. In every story the guildknight of Mithrandon remains neatly silent as the ocean and faceless as the wind. No one describes what lies beneath the armor. Some go on to say no one has ever seen what that polished metal shell concealed. The guildknight of these stories seems to have burst from the earth itself, as though lightning split a rock and out jumped a creature already clad in the accoutrements of the Imperial hunting guild. After all, these tales are really about good versus evil, about the triumph of the will, about the indomitable strength of the servants of the Sun Empire. What does it matter who is at the center of them? In their tellings, the masked guildknight never shows any weakness. They are never hurt and they are always victorious. As they should be.

But we know better, of course. How could we not? We, who are kin to the dragons, surely know the names of our own grandmothers and of the lives they led. Listen now to this tale, written the way it was told to us by our foremothers, who in turn learned it from their own foremothers.

Hear now the tale of Kunlin Yeva. Hear now the truth of the guildknight of Mithrandon.

CHAPTER TWO

TO BEGIN WITH, we must travel to the past.

Kunlin Yeva was thirteen when she slew her first dragon. The hero's feat comes to her unexpectedly: her mother is months away on business, and her father left that morning to hunt. The dragon comes into the kitchen where her little sister, Beyar, sits alone, and Yeva, drawing water from the well, hears her scream. On instinct she runs for her father's sword in the shed. In the kitchen she finds disaster: jars smashed, stools upended, milk spilled over stone. On the counter, the dragonling hisses with smoke and fury. A scrawny creature, freshly hatched, all nerve and plate and bone. Blue scales with a faint rainbow sheen, and a pale belly not yet armored. Yeva puts herself between the dragon and Beyar, fear-frozen in a corner, shouting, "Begone!" in hopes that it might bolt out the door.

The dragon instead lunges at her. As Beyar howls, Yeva fights it off, swinging her weapon with wild abandon. Her father has been teaching her the sword since last summer, but everything she knows has fled her, and she slaps it atop the head as though using a broom, striking it with the flat side of the blade. The dragon swipes and the sword goes clattering to the ground. Yeva staggers and falls as the dragon leaps upon her and fastens its teeth in the flesh of her wrist, grinding her bones and setting a fire. It will not let go and she cannot pull it off. Blood runs over her hands and arm, a startling color, like jam. Her vision goes prickly and a buzz swells in her head, and she realizes this might be the moment of her death. But that thought is distant, as if behind a pane of glass.

The dragon has small yellow eyes and horns that are still budding, covered in velvet. The muscles in its neck twitch as it adjusts its grip. Yeva watches her blood seep between the treads of its teeth. What does it think as it takes the life from her? It, too, is in a struggle for survival. The burning in her flesh grows weighty as it spreads to her chest, as if she could wield it, pick it up, and swing it around like a hammer. Blue fire coats her arm. At first Yeva thinks it came from the dragon, but the creature shrinks in fear from the tongues of flame. It lets go and scuttles away. Impossible strength fills Yeva's limbs, and she stands, thinking she has to kill the dragon now or she will never get the chance. Covered in strange fire, she picks up the dragonling as it tries to run, and snaps its neck with one quick twist. Its bones crackle like a broken twig. Yeva thinks nothing of it, as though she'd just crushed a tick or killed a hen for supper. She is still quite dizzy, and as she steps forward, arm dripping blood, the ground tilts under her and she faints.

Her father, Paul, returns home to disaster: one daughter out of her mind with fear in a ruined kitchen, the other on the floor with a maimed arm and a dragon whelp dead beside her. Yeva still lives, breathing shallowly, but Paul sees the marks of blue fire on her and around her. He knows what it means: the thing that he had prayed to never happen has indeed come to pass.

When Yeva wakes, tearing through a veil of darkness heavy and close as an ocean, she finds her father sitting by her sickbed, his face long and grave. "I have sent for the guildknights," he said. "You must go north with them, to Mithrandon."

"Have I done something wrong?" she asks.

He sighs, and looks sadder than she's ever seen him. "No. You did everything exactly right. But you have my family's blood, and my family's gift with it, or so it seems. Some call it a curse. The guild will take you and train you. It is your destiny to become a wyrmslayer after all. I dearly wish it weren't so."

"Your family's gift?" Her wounded hand throbs under the coverlet, and Yeva is afraid to look. "You never speak of your family."

"And with good reason."

Yeva hesitates, thinking of Beyar. Trying to form a counterargument, not realizing that her father's mind is already made and she has as much chance at convincing the sun not to set. "Mithrandon's so far away." Mithrandon is where the Emperor lives, where her father comes from. Their village lies on the edge of the His Radiance's influence, which the long shadow of the Imperial capital barely touches. Yeva has only heard stories of the city; when she tries to picture it, there's nothing. Emptiness, fuzzy as wool.

"You won't be alone," her father says. "My brother lives in Mithrandon. The Baron Deerland. He's a guildmaster, he'll be your patron."

"Your brother? By blood?" In her father's stories, he was a simple wanderer from the north who found love and settled here, the humblest of tales. Yeva never knew he was of noble birth. "Does he know who I am?"

Paul sighs. "You're blood. He'll take you in." He does not sound convinced.

"You've always said blood doesn't matter."

"It doesn't," he says. "Until it does."

This is not a decision her father should be making alone; it is not his choice to make. Later, in her letters, Yeva's mother will lament that, had she been present, she would not have allowed her daughter to go to the north. She understands more of magic than Paul did. She could have taught Yeva herself. But if she hadn't been away, she would have handled the dragon, and Yeva's gifts might never have been discovered. Paul is simply a mortal man who, fragile in his fear, reached first for that which was comforting to him. Despite it all, he is still a son of the Empire's capital city.

The pair of guildknights who come for her are gruff but kind, and speak little to her except to give direction. They have her father's pale complexion and eyes the color of leaves or jewels, and wear identical livery in red and white. Beyar fills a small sack with biscuits and dry breads for the long journey ahead. Yeva says, "I will write often, when the doctors in the city have healed my hand. Father can read them to you." Her sister nods, face pinched as she tries not to cry.

During their monthlong journey to Mithrandon, Yeva and her chaperones remain cordial strangers to one another. Yeva learns to eat with her left hand as her right one stiffens into a hook she can barely bend at the wrist. At night, when they think she is asleep, the guildknights whisper to one another in her father's language, which she understands, although not well. Yeva drinks in their gossip, despite not knowing who or what they are talking about. The inscrutability of their lives and concerns troubles her.

Mithrandon accosts her with its clamor and filth. The cobbled streets are flanked by stone-gray buildings inlaid with colored glass, and everywhere she looks there are people, constellations of busy lives intertwined. She feels dizzy imagining how each shuffling figure she passes has a name that she does not know and probably never will.

The walls of the guild fortress enclose the only silence in the city. Yeva feels her anxiety subside as they ride past stone courtyards speckled with guildknights in the red-and-white that has, by this point, become a source of comfort, of dependability. At the stables, she sees her first-ever gryphon, a gray-green stallion that pins her with its unblinking gaze, perceiving her—muddy tunic and all—as an intruder.

Her uncle's office requires a climb of innumerable steps. The room has impossibly high ceilings and more books than she's ever seen, and ever expected to see, in her life. Yeva stands before a man who wears a copy of her father's face. His lip curls as he stares her up and down. "So he did it, after all."

She guesses that "he" means her father, Paul. The man continues: "Pity you take after that woman, despite carrying our exalted blood."

Heat rushes to her cheeks and up her neck. Yeva has never thought of her mother with anything but pride; her father often remarks admiringly how much they look alike, with their dark hair and golden skin. Immediately after, he would add that blood doesn't mean anything, that family is more than blood. She always thought it was for Beyar's sake, but now she's not so sure.

Her uncle says, "My disgrace of a brother claims you've slain a dragon. Have you proof of that?"

Yeva has brought the dragon's bones in a bag. They clatter in a meager pile as she upends the bag over a table in the attached study. Her uncle sifts through them with a pale, thin finger, lips thinning as the curved yellow ribs knock into one another. "You call this a dragon? 'Tis barely a worm. If we accepted every lowly farmer who cut one apart with a spade, we'd be overrun."

Yeva thinks that any farmer who killed a beast like the one that maimed her should be allowed to be a guildknight if they so wish. She recalls the nighttime whisperings of her chaperones, their pointed barbs. "And you, sir? How many dragons have you slain?"

Her uncle's face darkens. In the shadows, someone giggles. A boy, not much older than her, has been hiding between two bookshelves. He covers his mouth instantly, but the damage has been done. "You," says her uncle, pointing. "If you've time enough to lounge about eavesdropping, you've time enough to be useful. Take this one to the quartermaster and get her sorted."

Yeva follows the thin boy down labyrinthine passageways, their footsteps swallowed up by the curved shoulders of the fortress. "My name's Emory," he says. "Did I hear correctly what my father said? Are you Sepaul's daughter? If so, that makes us cousins."

Yeva nods, overwhelmed by the sudden, casual appearance of a new relative. Emory says, "Sorry about my father. He's very set in his ways and can be quite blunt. Far too blunt, in fact. Some would say cruel. Do you have siblings, by the by?"

"I have a sister," she says. "Beyar. She's not of my father's blood, though. My mother found her abandoned and took her in. But she's my sister, all the same."

Emory nods thoughtfully. "You know, my father once considered adopting a boy with gifts like yours—a distant relative, but one of common birth—so that at least one of his heirs would have the sacred blood. But nothing came of it. He's got me, and nothing else. Is it nice, having a sibling?"

Yeva nods. "It is."

"I see. You should tell me stories of your home, if you have the time. I like to hear about faraway places."

He hops from topic to topic like a bird, bursting with curiosity. She has already decided that she likes Emory, who seems unbearably soft in this world of stone and hard angles. Mithrandon will be endurable, she thinks, if they can become friends. Later that day, when he brings her new clothes to wear, she notices that his cheek is reddened, as if recently struck. He sees her staring and smiles, sheepish. "Father gets mean when he's had too much to drink," he says, as if that is a reasonable explanation. Yeva feels—and knows—that this has something to do with what she said earlier, her insolence rippling outward invisibly, in ways she had not predicted. It is the first lesson she's learned in Mithrandon, and in many ways it is the most important one.

They send her to the infirmary first. In the cold light of the stone room, Yeva sits nervously as the guild doctor examines her. He takes the stiff claw of her hand, river-bright with scar tissue, and turns it this way and that, making chicken noises with his tongue. The doctor's age is marked by his silver hair and the white talons of battle-wounds across his face. In his youth, he was a wyrmslayer of great renown, and he has seen it all, every injury, every form of death. "This should have been looked at months ago," he says, "when it was still tender. Now the bones and sinew have set. It is healed."

"Can't you undo it?" Yeva asks.

Yeva gets irritation in response. The doctor vanishes into the next room, leaving Yeva alone under the domed roof of the infirmary, heart pounding, half-filled with hope and half-filled with dread. He returns with a gilt box, and inside is something which catches Yeva by surprise: a silver dagger with a sword's pommel too long for something so small. The blade itself is unusual, shaped like a splash of water, frozen. A thin stripe of blue crystal runs down the middle of the handle. "Can you hold this?"

Yeva works her broken hand around the pommel, the crystal digging into the thickened skin of her palm. As she lifts the dagger she feels her chest tighten, and she is back in her mother's house again, in the ruined kitchen, dizzy with unknown power. The blade comes to life, completing itself in a flash of blue, and Yeva sees that it is a sword after all, and the metal is only a scaffolding for the fire her father said is their family's birthright.

"Very good," says the doctor. "If you can wield a sword, then the hand's not useless. There's nothing to change."

"But what about letters?" Yeva asks, putting the sword down.

He looks irritated again. "What about them?"

"How will I write letters home? I promised—"

"If you have letters to write, you may employ a scribe," he says dismissively. "Home ... what need of letters have they, anyway? What would they understand of the affairs of knights?"

Yeva's stomach roils at the thought of all the tender words she wants to send to Beyar, to her parents, being passed through the hard end of a scribe's nib. The doctor sees the look on her face and says, "Better for you to forget them back home. Your life is given to the Sun Emperor, to serve at his pleasure. The guild is your family now."

In this way Yeva comes to understand the way her new family sees her: as a blade, an object whose value lies in serving His Radiance. When she is introduced to the other knights-in-training, she also comes to understand that her gift is exceedingly rare, that most guildknights work in pairs or teams, and are just as likely to perish against a full-grown dragon as they are to survive. The blade the doctor had her hold is a relic, a sacred weapon, and the blue crystals it bears are everstone, a catalyst that draws directly from the gift in Yeva's blood. The others can't wield it. From the beginning, she is already set apart from them. Then there are the other things: her foreignness, her maimed hand, the way her face looks like none of theirs. The lot are boys, mostly, and have a tower all to themselves, while Yeva's room is in the scullery with the maids. None of the trainees are openly cruel to her, but Yeva feels the cruelty in them nonetheless, in their glances and their whispers behind her back. If she leaves her gauntlets unattended during training, they go missing and turn up in a ditch later. The first few weeks, Yeva cries herself to sleep at night. She dreams of her mother coming to bring her home, of her fearless mother kicking down the mortared flint of the fortress, picking her up by the neck, and swooping up into the sky. But Yeva knows her mother would be disappointed if she were broken by simple hardship. "You have the strength of the earth in you," she used to tell her daughters. "The rains can come and the ploughs can carve through you and still you will remain."

So Yeva persists. She takes to her studies with a fervor that surprises even her teachers. She learns to tame gryphons, reading the movements of their glossy feathered torsos between her heels until she can control their arcs in the air with the barest nudge. Her skill with the sword grows beyond reproach. She learns to wield the flames that are her family's birthright, practicing with the doctor's relic until she is good enough to warrant her own.

Yeva eats the soft, mealy food of the kingdom until she forgets that there are other textures, other flavors. Little by little, her mouth gets used to speaking her father's language until it becomes second nature, until those syllables dominate even her thoughts and the language she spoke in her mother's home fades and becomes brittle in her mind. In the evenings, when Emory's personal tutoring is over, she dictates letters home in her new native tongue, and he dutifully writes them down. She knows she will never again be able to send word in her home language.

As the days pass, Yeva spends increasing stretches of time in the garb of the guildknights, finding comfort in the regularity of its appearance, an assurance that she belongs. The golden masks they wear while training make a secret of her face, while the reinforced leather conceals the markers of her sex. She looks no different from the other knights-to-be, except she is swifter and fiercer. She learns quicker and works harder. Yeva practices drills alone until dusk, until she is forced to retire to bed, where she sleeps restless hours until she can wake and put on her training garb again. Routine grows into habit, until Yeva can no longer imagine appearing beyond the walls of her room without her armor.

Sooner than expected, the day arrives where the swordmasters declare Yeva ready to join the ranks of the full guildknights. She has worked hard and her diligence has borne fruit. There is nothing more they can teach her; very soon, she should expect to be sent out on her first mission.

Her father, now living alone in a southern city, sends her a wyrmhound pup in congratulations. Emory commissions the forging of a new everstone weapon, Varuhelt, its blade longer than Yeva is tall. He presents it to her in the room where they first met, under the narrow scrutiny of his father. Yeva hefts the silver hilt, engraved with the serpentine body of a southern dragon whose open mouth gives the impression that it spits the blue flame that makes up the sacred blade. It is beautiful, perfectly balanced, perfectly smithed to fit in Yeva's clawlike hand. As Yeva raises it over her head and wakes it, a bolt of azure fire fills the room with harsh light as though touched by the goddess herself.

The guild tailors fit Yeva for the full garb of a guildknight in a vast room rimmed with mirrors of glass. A dozen apprentices bustle around her like fish in a river, robing her in mail and leather and dragonplate, taking measurements and pinning excess fabric, while their master grunts and gestures for adjustments. As they tug the red-and-white livery into place, Yeva looks out of the slits of her visor and sees, in the looking-glass, the perfect image of a guildknight being dressed by their attendants, no different from the knights who stride through the courtyards of the fortress, who stand in lines when His Radiance comes to visit. She could be anyone; no one can tell that she is the strange broken yellow girl intruding upon the ranks of the kingdom's finest.

That realization bursts in her chest like a warm sun. Within the shell of armor she feels, for the first time since leaving home, that she belongs where she is, that there is nothing wrong with her. Taken from the soil and cradle of her home and placed in this hard land, full of stone and bright metal, she has fashioned a womb for herself from which she can safely navigate her new world. It is at this moment that Yeva makes her vow—a pledge not to the goddess or the Emperor but to herself. She will remain within this shell of leather and metal forevermore. No more shall she suffer the judgment of others who will look into her face and find it lacking. No more shall she seem like an interloper, an unworthy stranger squatting within the holiest walls of the Sun Empire. From this day on, people should look at her and see nothing but a faithful servant of Mithrandon, pure in ability and beyond reproach. She knows the road ahead will be difficult, and its many impracticalities will test her will. But she is determined to triumph over such banalities, obstacles of mortar and flesh. In the days to come, the immense bulk of the armor will cease to feel like an oppressive hand pressing down upon her head, and more like the arms of the goddess, holding her in a protective embrace. Keeping her dear and close to the bosom of the Empire so that she may not stray. Yeva falls into this fate with her eyes shut and her arms wide open. Never looking back at what she has left behind.

CHAPTER THREE

AND NOW WE jump ahead, to a time when the Sun Empire is in its heyday. Picture Mithrandon: City of knights and emperors, city of lofty dreams, city of heroes and fantastical deeds. City that does not wake and does not sleep, city that turns like a millhouse wheel and spins all of the world in its gyre. City to which all eyes of the glorious, sprawling Thrandic Empire turn. City to which all bow their grateful heads. In the heart of this city lives the white-walled guildknight's fortress, its cheek nestled against the mighty bulwark of the Imperial castle.

And in the heart of this fortress lives the famed masked guildknight, going about her morning ablutions as she has for the last dozen years. A thousand mornings Kunlin Yeva has woken in the same round stone room, and a thousand mornings she conducts the same precise ritual. By Yeva's own choice she employs no staff. Once, she asked if her little sister could come to Mithrandon to serve as her lady-in-waiting, but her mother forbade it so vehemently she never asked again. In place of help, Yeva has learned self-reliance, so that tasks which require a coterie of maids and attendants can be done alone with one maimed hand that can hold little but a sword.

The garb of a guildknight comprises layer upon layer, which she puts on in front of the bronze mirror and washbasin aided by a series of connected hooks and pulleys designed for the very purpose of holding the pieces still. First, the leggings of worsted wool and a shirt of stiff linen. A halter to hold her chest in place. Then the plain white doublet, lined with silk, impermeable to arrows. Over it, she fastens a gusset of mail so fine it feels like cotton. On top of that, the surcoat of bright red with the heraldry of the guild, held around her waist by a thin belt of leather. Now the gloves of supple calfskin, stitched with emblems in gold thread. Leather shoes. And finally, over her head, obscuring her features, the padded silver helm with its plume of red, without which her bones feel unnaturally light, as if she might be swept off by a breeze. Only then does she look complete in the bronze mirror, all silk and metal, neither trace of hair nor hide showing. Only then does she feel comfortable in leaving the room.

Even amongst the ranks of the exalted guildknights Yeva carries an aura of mystery, an almost mythic air. Few know her name and even fewer have seen her face. To the others, Yeva's age, background, and gender are open to speculation, which fresh recruits take to like swans upon water. But once the days and months gather about them, once they've been sent out for a hunt or two, their curiosity fades and the masked guildknight becomes yet another installation in their regimented lives, their unknowability reliable as the pillars that make up their fort. A revered elder whose capabilities set them apart, whose existence is undeniable, but whose humanity is unobserved and unknown. Yeva does not mind. She does not care.

At the tail end of winter, as the days are slowly beginning to brighten again, the guildmaster sends for Yeva. He bears important instructions, although at that time neither of them realize how much weight these edicts carry, and how their presence will tilt the balance of their world. Yeva, suspecting nothing at all, makes her way to the office at the top of the fortress's command tower with neither hesitation nor trepidation.

The master of the guildknights is a peculiar man even when accounting for the eccentricities of the rich and powerful. Emory Deerland has grown into a kinder, softer man than his father before him, and the guildknights have flourished under his guidance. But this does not stop the dukes and captains of the Emperor's regular armies from indulging in gossip about this thin, strange man who can barely draw a bow and would rather spend his hours with his nose in a dusty tome, or bent over a desk fiddling with little gears and prongs. If this bothers Emory, he does not show it. Yeva admires this about him. If only she could be so adamantine, with thick skin and a hard heart without the need to resort to hiding in metal. While the other guildknights are arranged in companies that report to a captain, and those captains report to the guildmaster, Yeva takes no orders except from Emory, answers to no one except for him.

Emory's receiving boy, Telken, lets her up the stairs to his office, warning that his master is busy with a project. This is nothing new; Emory is the sort who cannot keep his hands still. The troubles of running the Emperor's elite hunting forces often fail to keep his mind sufficiently occupied, so he makes up his own amusement. Each time Yeva ascends the circular stairs and steps into his office, she is never sure what she will find. Once he filled the receiving space with huge boards upon which he'd tacked sheaves of parchment as he tried to translate an ancient text from Elkandar. Another time he'd built an elaborate clockwork opera that played tinny music and had twirling dancers in enameled dresses, a gift for a young nobleman he fancied. But today, instead of dead languages or romantic gestures, there's an elaborate metal cylinder laid on the work desk like a fresh specimen, long as a human arm, bristling with copper filaments and wirework. Emory is bent over it, a mask with crystal eyeglasses fixed to his face, utterly absorbed with his pins and tweezers. Beside him is a sealed glass box containing a blue crystal the size of an acorn. Yeva recognizes it as the sacred everstone that makes the blue flame of her weapon.

Emory doesn't look up as Yeva arrives with her metallic footsteps. She doesn't interrupt him as he fusses over the metalwork. A companionable silence curls up in the room as Yeva waits, patient.

Something audibly clicks into place and Emory grunts in satisfaction. As he picks up a different grade of tweezers he murmurs, "I read your report on Callenden. Very interesting. We really don't know much about how dragons breed. All my research seems to indicate that laying eggs is extremely rare. We hardly ever hear about dragon nests, but there are plenty of stories of dragons being born through spiritual means. Some even say that dragons might take on human form to give birth to live young. Of course it's hard to sort out which part is fact and which is fiction when dealing with mythology, but at the same time so much of these creatures' lives are mythical. Even to us, who make a living off culling them. And there are so many different kinds of dragon too."

While he rambles, Emory puts down his tools and hinges open a chamber on the side of the cylinder. Carefully, he unseals the glass box containing the everstone and picks it up with a pair of tongs.

"I brought egg fragments back," Yeva says.

"Yes, and Doctor Haskyn has positively exploded in excitement. I expect he'll be busy with his new specimens for several months." He places the crystal into the chamber and closes the lid. Nothing happens, and he frowns.

"You haven't summoned me just to talk about what happened at Callenden."

"No. No, I haven't." Emory sighs, putting his tools aside and pushing up his mask. The leather and glass have left marks on his pale face. "Yeva, I'm sending you to Quentona."

"Quentona?" She frowns under her helm as the wheels turn slowly in her mind. She knows that place by a different name, Quanbao. A kingdom to the south, close to where she was born and grew up. "Into a foreign land? Have they requested aid?"

"That, I cannot say." Another deep sigh as Emory gets up and goes to his writing desk. He retrieves a golden scroll from a stand on his desk and smooths it over a clean expanse with careful fingers. "Our esteemed Sun Emperor, profound in his wisdom and bountiful in friendship," he recites, "is commissioning a garrison of special agents to be sent to protect the neighboring land of Quentona in a gesture of brotherhood. His Radiance has been troubled by recent reports by patrols in the south of a great and terrible storm dragon that batters the mountains of Quentona, unopposed and unabated. In his generous heart he has decreed that we shall lend aid to our neighbors, who have no guildknights like we do, and are thus unable to defend against a threat so dire."

"But this is ridiculous." The broad wings of the Thrandic Empire have great span, from the highlands of Gudbyar in the north to the wet plains of Chushang in the south, where she hails from. Quanbao—or Quentona, as the Emperor names it—is beyond those borders, a place where knights of the Empire have no jurisdiction. "Have they in Quanbao—in Quentona—have they asked His Radiance for such a favor?"

Emory rolls the Emperor's edict into a tight curl and drops it into its stand with an audible clatter. "That is beyond my ken, Yeva. All I know is what the Emperor has asked."

But of course Emory understands the Emperor's desires. Even Yeva does, and she is a brute who knows little beyond the ways of the sword. Emory, with his smarts, with all the books and knowledge he has swallowed, surely sees that the Emperor is looking for a toehold into the next region over. It's been a while since they've had a war. His armies are idle and His Radiance is bored.

Emory says, "There was a hunt on the border of Quanbao a number of years ago. Before you came to us. Not too long before, in fact. The dragon gave us the slip and fled toward Quanbao, crossing the border. The Emperor believes that same dragon lives in Quanbao still and will one day return to exact his revenge. Or so he says. He was a child when this happened."

Unease grows within Yeva like a toothache. During her childhood her mother often left for weeks at a time to visit Quanbao's capital. Wasn't it during one such trip that Yeva's tragedy occurred and she was taken away to Mithrandon? Over the passage of years Yeva has put aside all thoughts of her home village and its reclusive neighbor. Now, the thought of the Sun Emperor turning his hungry gaze upon that peaceful, remote land fills her with soaring alarm.

Slowly and flatly she says, "They worship dragons in Quanbao. I cannot imagine they would seek His Radiance's aid in such matters."

"Nor can I," Emory says.

Yeva's breaths collect in her helm, dense and humid. In her mind she puts pieces of information together. "The King of Quanbao died last year, and her daughter has yet to ascend the throne."

"Yes. The kingdom seems to be in a position of some vulnerability, doesn't it?"

"So what will you do? Will you refuse His Radiance's order?"

"Of course not." He frowns at this ludicrous idea. "Not unless I want to be exiled. I've already said—Yeva, I'm sending you instead. He wants a company of men stationed in

Quentona. I don't want that. His Radiance wants to manufacture an incident, a shallow pretext to send in the armies he so happily built up over the last recruiting season. I won't let him use us as his blunt tool. Sending a single elite guild-knight is a good compromise."

Ice sags in her belly. "You mean to send me there—to live? For how long?"

"For as long as His Radiance wants. But his attention will waver eventually."

"So you mean months. Years."

Her cousin shakes his head. "Yeva, it's a lot to ask. I know. But, beyond your unparalleled skill with the sword, there is more to you which suits this mission. Who else within the guild has connections to that land like you do? Sending the others, sending some pack of brutes would be like loosing a raging bull into a garden."

"I know nothing of that land. I have not returned home in a dozen years. I might as well be a stranger to it, no different from the other knights."

"But you *are* different."

This line, said so simply and plaintively by her cousin, slugs her below the chest. Perhaps he meant it a different way than Yeva understood it, but it wounds her all the same.

Still, the hurt is invisible beneath her armor, and Emory clatters onward, oblivious. "I have no confidence that the other guildknights will behave themselves, or treat the girl-king of Quentona with the respect she deserves. I fear that sending any of them will be the cause of so much offense that, over time, conflict between our nations will become inevitable. Yeva, I ask you to do this because I trust you like no other. You are my dearest cousin, and I know you have a gentle hand. I will feel better if you are there, instead of anyone else.

"After all," he adds, "it'll almost be like a homecoming for you, won't it?"

Yeva shudders. Despite everything, over the years she has managed to carve out a place where she belonged within the guild, in Mithrandon. A hard-won belonging she is now expected to abandon for a strange land, under strange circumstances. To be alone and nobody again. And Emory can't see how much his request is asking of her. He even thinks this will be better for her.

But in the end, she—Kunlin Yeva—is a blade that falls at the convenience of the guild; the desires of captain and empire must outweigh what desires she has. "If that is what you wish," she simply says, and Emory brightens, glad for her cooperation. She stays silent as he immediately begins making plans aloud, laying down the minutiae of sending her abroad, all while she is trying to imagine waking up in a foreign space, in a room that is not hers, in a distant land where she has never been, and feeling small and invisible.

Emory hasn't noticed. He's still talking about sending messengers ahead.

Once upon a time, her father fled Mithrandon for the south, bursting from a life of comforts and plenty into an uncertain fate. Yeva has always wanted to know what that journey felt like, but she has never wondered about it as hard as she does now.

Enough is enough. Yeva crushes her sorrow into a seed smaller than the palm and buries it deep within herself. Perhaps later, when this is all over, she will allow it to sprout. But for now, she knows her duty. She is, after all, a magnificent, faceless blade of the guild. Like clockwork she, too, moves when her springs are wound. She will go to Quentona.

CHAPTER FOUR

QUANBAO—QUENTONA—IS a half-year's journey by foot and a month away on horseback. Soaring through blue skies in a gryphon carriage, Yeva closes the gap in two days.

A range of craggy mountains stands on the border between the kingdom of Quentona and the Sun Empire, split by the Zochar Pass, a fissure through which a single stony road winds into the heart of the kingdom. On her way to the pass, Yeva sails over the pastures and paddies of her old home and a seam of longing opens between her ribs. How many years has it been? A memory breaks through like the first buds of spring, all smells and tastes: the smoke of her mother's kitchen, the piquant caramel of a stuffed pork bun melting in her mouth. But the picture in her mind is incongruous: she's thinking of a child with limbs like brown twigs, a smile as wide as her face. Yeva hasn't looked or acted like that for years.

A wall of wooden palisades outlines Quentona's borders. The guard at the gate scowls suspiciously at the Imperial scroll Yeva presents him, but it is not for him to refuse an envoy of the Thrandic Emperor. To do so would be to oppose the will of the Emperor, and His Radiance has historically not taken kindly to such matters. Before Yeva, massive wooden doors with hand-whittled lotus-flower reliefs creak inward, heavy and oaken, and she follows the path up into the mist and gray of Quentona.

Despite her proximity to it, Yeva has never been across the border. In her childhood Quentona was simply the neighboring kingdom, shrouded and mysterious, a place her mother went to on trips with other elders. She has never met anyone from there; the impression Quentona gives is of a small and fiercely reclusive nation, protected by unforgiving terrain and bristling with strange customs. Even her mother, so generous with her tales of the sun and the sea and the sky, hardly spoke of her trips up the mountains—it was grown-up business and Yeva was not yet grown. "But when you're older," she used to promise, "I will take you with me. One day you will learn everything I know." In the years since Yeva went to Mithrandon, the image of Quentona has faded into a haze of ambiguity, something which was once important to her childish, hopeful heart, brushed away by the hard practicalities of the world.

This is all she knows about the kingdom in the present: half as many people dwell in the entire country as do live in any small town in the Empire; its rule is matrilineal, unlike the way it is in Mithrandon; the current monarch is young, a girl-king, someone who inherited the position when her mother died a year ago. Fat tongues of ore crisscross the mountains that make up the land; fine steel and silver are among the country's biggest exports, sold in exchange for dark wines and cotton and ripe, plump fruit. Yeva understands why His Radiance, with all his childlike greed, wants this prize for his own.

The stony road leads her to Daqiao, the country's capital, resting upon the flank of a mountain just inside the border. An imposing wall of gray brick stands around it, and its entrance is a pair of bloodred doors with golden studs, tall and wide enough for a dragon to fly through. An official in indigo robes allows her passage into the city. His scowl is even deeper than his border guard counterpart's.

The streets beyond the city gates are almost too narrow for Yeva's gold-and-white carriage. She drives slowly and cautiously through these winding paths that look nothing like the ones she's familiar with. Wooden buildings with sloping roofs line either side. She causes disruption as she goes, her passage a wound that closes up behind her. Glimpses of color and delight are snatched out of her sight as soon as she gets close.

Her golden scroll grants her passage to the outskirts of the royal palace, circled by walls covered in glittering mosaic. Mythical creatures dance among swirls of azure cloud. The palace is split in two: a lower half at street level where the stables and civil servants are, and an upper half where the girl-king and the palace servants live. Yeva is swept into the no-nonsense care of the palace guard, who want to assign her attendants, sleeping quarters, a stable hand to take care of her gryphons. She rejects all this. "I sleep in my carriage," she says. "And my gryphons will not tolerate the touch of those who are not their master. I will tend to them myself."

The captain of the guard is a man named Lu, whose face holds a map's worth of frown lines. "You cannot be serious," he says. His Mithrandish is heavily accented. "We cannot allow an esteemed guest of Lady Sookhee's to sleep in the stables. A preposterous idea! Anyone would think that we were meaning to cause offense to the Sun Emperor's envoy."

"There will be no offense taken."

"We must insist."

"This is not a test," Yeva says, more snappily than intended. She has been in Quanbao for less than an hour and already things are difficult. "I wish to sleep in my carriage. It's what I find comfortable."

The look on Captain Lu's face tells her that there was offense taken, and it was on his end. She realizes too late that it sounds like an insult on the quality of the accommodations in the royal palace. It's too late to take it back. An hour in and already she has fallen short of what Emory expects.

So Yeva sets up in a corner of the royal stables, taking it over with the bulk of her carriage. She turns the gryphons loose and lets her wyrmhound, Sage, out of the carriage to stretch her legs. The pup kicks up dirt as she inscribes loops around the courtyard, fueled by pent-up energy. A pair of stablehands—one an old man with flyaway cotton hair and one a skinny kid no older than twelve—stare at the enormous winged beasts with a mixture of curiosity and terror.

"They won't harm you," Yeva says. "If you don't bother them, they won't harm you."

Neither of them speak or acknowledge what she said. She realizes they might not speak her language. This is going to be difficult.

Captain Lu returns near sundown. "You must be famished from your long journey. Is this venerable knight of Mithrandon too proud to eat dinner with the peons of the royal guard?"

Yeva hesitates, suddenly trapped. To refuse would be to offer further insult, and yet Yeva hasn't shared a meal with others since she was a child. "I cannot remove this helm in public. It is forbidden. I must therefore dine alone."

The captain scoffs, his patience with her worn thin. "Very well. If you wish to eat in the stables like a dog, who am I to argue?"

Soon after, a woman in seafoam-green silk with peach accents arrives bearing several woven baskets with lids. The baskets contain an array of food so dizzying it might feed an army: fried and boiled dishes, baskets of steamed confections, oily bowls of soup. Crystal-skin dumplings, whole fried snakehead, double-boiled soup with lotus root and groundnut, stewed winter melon, crispy whitebait, pastry shells filled with shrimp and radish salad. On and on.

Yeva, overwhelmed, takes the baskets into her carriage and shuts herself in. Each of the dishes comprises a small serving, almost too small—two mouthfuls and they're gone. The flavors punch her in the throat, heavy on her tongue and bright on the roof of her mouth. Yeva forces herself to eat slowly, to savor every note, from the sweetness of the dumplings to the rich salt-and-bitter of lotus root soup. Familiar ropes of aroma drag her back in time until she stands within the walls of her mother's house, stirring a pot of fish stock, breathing in the thick and pungent steam. Yeva closes her eyes and steeps herself in these feelings, while at her feet Sage whines for leftovers.

Her time here will be fraught and she might not survive it. She's barely set foot in the nation and already she feels unstable and anxious, as if she might tilt and fall unexpectedly into the earth with every step. Tombs long sealed will be broken open, and Yeva is afraid of what she will find buried within.

※

LADY SOOKHEE, THE girl-king of Quentona, is ill. She has been for a long time, with a blood-sickness that flares up and subsides with alarming regularity. Yeva has arrived during one of those resurgences, while she is too frail to receive visitors. Words could not express her deep regret at such impropriety, but she is afraid that the esteemed knight of Mithrandon must wait before she can formally welcome her.

All this Yeva finds out from a silk scroll brought to her in the morning by a different woman in peach and seafoam green. The Thrandish in the missive is flawless and formal, written in a neat but strange hand. The blotty shape of the letters indicates use of an ink-dipped brush instead of a sharp nib; peculiar, but beautiful. Dismay grows within Yeva as she reads the scroll over and over. Lady Sookhee does not say how long Yeva is expected to wait in this unsettled, suspended state before she can be formally assigned to court—or whatever the girl-king wishes to do with her. She only asks Yeva to trouble Captain Lu or Sujin—the handmaiden who has brought her the scroll—if she has any needs.

There's one more thing. Tied to the end of the scroll is a thin sliver of iridescent material braided within an elaborate decorative knot. A royal seal. Taken anywhere, this should allow Yeva patronage of any of the shops in the city, whether she should desire to try some of Daqiao's delicacies or stay at one of their famous hot-spring inns. If she is so inclined.

But Yeva is not. She looks to Sujin, a plump woman perhaps in her thirties, with an air of severity that suffers no fools. "What should I do, then?"

"How would I know? Do whatever you like, it's none of my business." She seems irked to be talking to a guest in the stables, this loud and unruly place. She pointedly keeps her distance from Yeva's carriage. When Yeva doesn't respond to what she said, she simply turns and leaves without a further word.

Yeva finds herself left alone and unattended. Time stretches before her like a desert, taunting her with its emptiness. In Mithrandon, she had routines to fill the spaces between hunts, but she is no longer in Mithrandon, and the idea of leisure seems offensive to her.

She examines the braided seal more closely. Its iridescent center, which has the appearance of hammered metal, shimmers and flexes irregularly. Yeva realizes she knows what it is: dragonscale. A sibling material to the sheets that make up her golden armor, though more like insect shell and less like steel. Dragonscale comes in varieties as diverse as the beasts they are carved from, and this scale is novel to her, from a type of dragon she's never seen before.

A shiver passes through Yeva. She's certain she isn't wrong; nothing else in the natural world carries the aura this scale has. The blood in her hand fizzes as she brushes her fingertip against it: her sacred gift reacting, responding to the traces of divinity left in the material. The more attention she pays to it, the sharper the sensation becomes. Why is dragon shed being used as a royal seal, and what does that mean? Might His Radiance be right about the threat of dragons living in Quanbao after all?

Yeva turns these questions over and over in her mind until a froth of suspicion builds around her thoughts. If there is some danger here, however slight, she must uncover it.

Within her carriage, in a finely tooled silver box that was a gift from Emory, she has stowed what information she could find about Quanbao. She unrolls the tight sheets of vellum and peruses their contents. There's not much to go on; what is available to her is sketchy and comprises a handful of patrol reports and dry summaries of the neighboring nation's military might. Emory could have found more by asking certain friends deep in the Imperial court with their fingers in the secret archives, but that would have taken time, and they did not have enough. So she makes do.

Most interesting is the account of a failed hunt on the edge of Quentona—Quanbao—more than a decade ago. Emory spoke of this. A guild party of six, pursuing a small southern dragon spotted near a village not twenty miles from where Yeva grew up. A winter sighting which went wrong, all but one of the party slipping in mud and falling into the river that borders the Empire and Quanbao along that point. The sole survivor was found by villagers days later, half-frozen and delirious, barely able to speak of what had happened. Yeva's attention is snared by the transcript of what he told Mithrandon's interlocutors weeks later, after he had been brought back to the capital:

> After a day and a night's hunt we cornered our foe on the banks of the river they call the Yalo. Its length was not greater than a six-boat, and its girth paltry besides; by its pale coloring and timid behavior our captain determined it to be a juvenile of its species (although it was of a sort that the guild has not yet fully recorded). Our champion, Aestafar, had grievously wounded it in its side with his greatsword. We felt assured of our victory and moved quickly. But in our certainty we failed to anticipate the true strength of our quarry. As it neared dusk, upon the riverbank, the infernal beast called up a great fog from the ground, through which we lost sight of it, and each other. A terrible chill descended upon us all, and a foul wind blew, but so thick lay the fog that it did not disperse even within the gale. The firmament turned to mud under us. Here my recollection falls prey to uncertainty: in the howling wind and stinging fog I cannot be sure of what I saw. I moved through the gloam, seeking out the rest of my party. I heard them cry out—I slipped in the mud—and then above me, a shadow so large it seemed like it might blot out the sun—the coil of some kind of creature, too large to have been the dragon we

were pursuing. Terror gripped me and I thought I was to meet my end. In my madness and desperation I thrust blindly upward with my lance, and the Sun Goddess must have been guiding my hand, for in the tempest I felt it strike something, almost like flesh. Blood rained upon me, a blue so dark it was almost black. The beast made a cry so awful I felt the ground might split and the world end. Strength fled me then, and as I lay in the cold mud I saw a dark, enormous shape fleeing toward the border of the neighboring nation. To what end, I do not know. I remember nothing more. That creature—it was no juvenile, but surely a demon dragged from the depths of the world, luring us in with its weakness before assuming its true form. Six of us there were, fine men all, and only I returned from that fateful encounter. I cannot fathom why Lady Eymthra protected me while my brothers-in-arms perished. . . .

The description of the hunt sends a chill through Yeva. It reads less like a knight's report than a tale of fantastical horror. Attached to the report is a note from the then-guildmaster—Baron Deerland, Emory's father—dismissing the man's report as a mere flight of fancy, touched in the head as he was after the death of his comrades.

Yeva does not know what to think. Clearly the Sun Emperor believes there is more to this story than the delirious ramblings of a madman. Or he doesn't. Possibilities and theories dance in Yeva's mind and gnaw at her sanity. There's little she can do to calm herself, but at the same time she feels too unsettled to remain alone in her carriage. And the thought of wandering the palace with its labyrinthine passages and dour servants sets her stomach roiling.

So she does the only thing she can think of: she leaves the palace to traverse the cobbled streets of Daqiao, in search of something she cannot name. Does she seek clues to a dragon's whereabouts? Is she looking for something more? She does not know and she cannot guess. Perhaps she simply seeks the simplicity that comes from walking, occupying herself with the simple effort of putting one foot in front of the other and deciding which way to turn. To silence her troubled mind, she carefully places her helm back over her head, retreating into a comfortable cocoon of safety. With the royal seal gripped in the gauntlet of her good hand, she steps out into an unfamiliar world, hoping to make it legible.

CHAPTER FIVE

A SOLDIER OF Mithrandon walks the streets of Daqiao. Heavy and faceless in her garb, her footfalls seem like an avalanche coming violently through the airy byways, punching through the merriment that fattens the air this early afternoon. It's lunchtime and the streets are bustling. Mothers haggle while children play skipping games in alleyways. A laborer, a stout young woman, walks past balancing bales of fragrant tea on her shoulders. Painted sign-cloths, drawn across the doorways of buildings, flutter in the wind. Yeva is furtive in the easygoing atmosphere of a market, unsure of its customs and anxious for purpose. Her feet lead her in unchartered directions. She cannot remember the last time she has explored a city as though a mere traveler—perhaps she never has. In this casual environment the armor she wears like a second skin starts to feel more like a cage, suffocating her and dimming her sight, making it hard to breathe.

Voices old and young call out from the stalls lining the streets, hawking their wares. The local tongue, which she has mostly caught as low fragments of a syllabary as officials whispered, now rushes around her like a rain-swollen river. Something about the lilt of those sounds opens a sweet well of familiarity in her mind so potent she feels intoxicated. She hears words that are almost like the language she spoke as a child. Words that haven't left her mouth since she went to Mithrandon. Yeva remembers her mother coming home from her trips to Quanbao with bagfuls of trinkets—a frog that sang when tilted, a cloisonné goldfish which rippled on the end of a rope like a living thing, a beautifully made lap zither—and a bosom full of wonderful stories and strange new knowledge. She always returned in high spirits, enervated by her trips to the neighboring country. In some stubborn crevice of her mind Yeva wants Daqiao to feel like another home, embracing her the way it once embraced her mother.

Would the citizens understand her if she spoke her mother tongue to them? Yeva wants to try. She approaches the closest stall, laden with jars of crystal honey and sticks of candied fruit. "Hello," she begins, haltingly. The words seem to come sideways out of her as she struggles to shape sounds she hasn't made for years. "What are you selling?"

The stallkeeper, a young man barely done growing, stares past her as if she's invisible. Perhaps he hasn't heard her. Yeva tries again. "Can you understand me?"

This time the man deliberately turns his head and barks

something at the neighboring stall. The portly woman in charge shakes her head and replies in the same unintelligible language, but Yeva knows sarcasm when she hears it. The two share a laugh.

The rebuke could not be clearer. But Yeva can't give up so easily. On impulse, hand trembling invisibly within her gauntlet, she flashes the braided seal to the young man. The dragonscale catches the light in tints of pink and blue. "Your king gave this to me," she says in Thrandish, thrusting it in his face. "Will you talk to me?"

The man's gaze drops to the scale, then back up to Yeva's face. His expression is inscrutable, his dark eyes like mirrors. She knows she's made a mistake—what was she thinking? The silence between them stretches until Yeva steps away, face burning with shrouded embarrassment. She feels the man's blank, accusatory gaze as she walks away, unable to blend into the crowd. Everywhere she goes a cushion of space opens up. Passersby take wider steps to avoid walking next to her. No one will meet her eyes. She walks among them a stranger, a threat sheathed in metal. A casual, careless sweep of her arm could destroy their wooden stalls and fragile buildings.

This denial hurts; her wish for Daqiao to be welcoming shattered as soon as she tries to bring it into reality. The city turns away from her. After all, why should the denizens of these streets know any better? They cannot see her and recognize her as a daughter of the land. All they see is the heraldry of the Empire. It is as though the child Yeva had once been never existed in the first place, and her fragmented memories of souvenirs from Daqiao are only delusions. Can she really be sure her mother ever came here? Is it not just wishful thinking?

The further she goes, the deeper into despair Yeva sinks. Inns and shops in the buildings wave her away or simply ignore her. Brandishing the girl-king's seal elicits silence, or questions in the local language she cannot answer. The solution, to her, seems obvious. Take off the helm, let them see that she isn't some marauding stranger who has come to threaten their country with Imperial power, let them see that she is a neighbor and a daughter to a woman who loved this city.

But that would be a lie. Yeva is every bit a marauding stranger from a foreign land, and the woman she is thinking of she has not spoken to for more than half her life. The idea of removing any part of her armor in public, revealing her visage to the world and the goddess in the skies above, turns her stomach. She cannot do it. It feels as impossible as asking her to sprout wings and fly.

Yeva is wasting her time. She should return to her carriage. The safety within that shell of wood and metal will not make her feel like a mistake for existing.

She turns and heads back up the street. Mired in gloomy

thought, she is startled when she hears someone call out in familiar words. "Knight from up north!"

A gray-haired woman leans in the doorway of an eatery she was too heartsick to bother trying. She gestures with a stiff hand. "Come here."

Her stomach drops again at the sound of the language she spoke at home. Yeva approaches slowly, trying to piece together what she knows of this woman. There's nothing familiar about her face, and yet—

"You're Douma's eldest, aren't you?"

Her heart leaps into her throat at the mention of her mother's name. Here it is, at last—a trace of her mother's journeys from her childhood, proof that her memories of childhood, and therefore Yeva herself, have not been so summarily erased from the rest of the world outside the walls of Mithrandon. "You know my mother? You know who I am?"

"Of course I do. Come."

The woman beckons her inside. Chest rushing with equal parts hope and fear, Yeva follows her instructions. She does not know what awaits her, but she cannot not know.

Sound spills over her as she steps inside: the clack of utensils, the burble of laughter. The ground floor bubbles with activity, every seat taken, every table laden with food. Wine is poured and oaths are sworn. A serving boy dodges past with a whole loin of crackle-skin pork laid upon a gleaming celadon plate, nimble on his feet despite the size of the dish.

The mysterious woman shouts instructions in Quanbao's language; somewhere in the depths of the eatery a hand waves in acknowledgement. Then, to Yeva: "Follow me."

Yeva feels two sizes too large in the building's cramped interior, stiff and bulky amongst these carefree civilians. Heads turn to stare at her, as though a guardian gargoyle has detached from its pedestal of stone to walk among them. Her chaperone heads up the stairs where it's quieter, leading them to a private room behind a paper-screen door. A long, low table has been set up with appetizers: sweet and spicy pickles, anchovy crisps, braised groundnuts. Embroidered cushions of silk line either side.

The woman doesn't sit down. She instead turns to Yeva. "Now. Will you take that silly helmet off?"

"I—" Yeva hesitates. Her heart works so hard in her chest it brings her pain. "I never take it off."

"What? They haven't glued it to your head, have they?"

"No, but—"

"Then take it off. How else are you going to eat?"

Yeva freezes. This stranger does not know what she's asking. The impossibility of wings, the fear of being seen outside the solid, protective walls of Mithrandon. She may as well have asked Yeva to boil her own flesh and turn into a dragon.

But—this woman knows Yeva's mother. She knows her

by name. She knew who Yeva was without seeing her face. If she refuses—if she turns tail and runs, fleeing back to the sanctuary of her carriage—she shall never know the story here. And perhaps she will curse herself to remain a stranger to all of Daqiao for as long as she is here.

She cannot do it. But she must do it.

Clumsily, hands almost unsteady, Yeva lifts the helmet off her head. She struggles at the task without the aid of her contraptions. But the damned thing eventually comes off, exposing her to a world that feels horribly bright and unrelenting. She squints on instinct, breathing the unrestrained air, pungent with grease and perfumed steam from the kitchens below.

The woman looks her up and down. "It is you," she says, nodding in satisfaction. "I see her in you. Clear as a spring pond."

Yeva gingerly draws in fresh air. The woman's gaze feels like hot coals upon her face. She thinks: This is what it feels like. This is what it's like to be normal. "How did you know my mother?"

She gestures to the table, brusque in her coyness. "Sit."

A serving girl brings them cups, a pot of tea, boiling water to wash the cups with. The woman begins to talk while she rinses the cups with the water and pours the tea. "You don't know me. Of course. My name is Anuya. I'm from the same village you were. Growing up, your mother and I were friends. Best friends, you could say. Then as a young woman I did what young women do and fell in love with a boy who passed through the village, and followed him home to Daqiao. Here I've been ever since."

"How did you know who I am?"

"I heard about you through gossip. How many girls from a small village like ours go off to the capital to become a heroic dragon-slaying knight? Everyone knows about the famous guildknight of Mithrandon. Even here in Daqiao."

Her offhand proclamation only worsens Yeva's anxiety; she imagines the hidden conversations people have had of her over the years and cannot imagine anything good has been said. Anuya glances at her face, her unshielded face, and laughs, finding amusement in Yeva's expressions. How do people live like this? Suddenly, Yeva doesn't want to talk about herself anymore.

She asks: "My mother used to come to Daqiao a lot. Was it to see you?"

"Ha!" Anuya sets one of the cups in front of Yeva. "If only! Your mother had much finer friends in this city. She was a confidante of the late King of Quanbao. Used to come in to give her counsel and everything." She catches sight of Yeva's round-eyed expression and snorts. "Didn't know that, did you?"

"She never told me. She said . . ." Yeva frowns. "*One day, when you're grown . . .*"

"Ah. Well, that sure sounds like Douma. Even as a child she was so full of secrets, always running off into the woods, learning magic and whatnot. When it turned out that she had royal favor in the neighboring kingdom, we weren't even surprised. Still . . . It was a scandal, you know, when you left for the north. In between Douma's reputation and who she married. Our village chief didn't approve of the union, but she did it anyway. She *loved* him, she said. Ah, look at the stupid things we do for love."

Yeva stares at the surface of the tea while her stomach quietly churns. Her family is a distant memory, and a happy one: warm afternoons in the fields and the laughter of her little sister as Yeva chases her. To hear these ugly secrets so casually dredged up by someone she doesn't know brings a wave of sourness to her mouth.

Anuya tuts. "You don't like tea? Your mother always ordered this."

Reluctant, she takes a sip. The tea is deep and smoky, with a woody fragrance that reminds her of incense burning. "It's a good brew." She thinks: my mother has good taste.

The screen door parts and the serving girl reappears with a tray: two bowls of chicken congee and a plate of stuffed pork buns. Simple. Delicious. The smell alone suffocates her with so much nostalgia she finds herself tearing up. "Eat, eat," Anuya says, waving generously at the dishes.

Yeva almost can't bear to. But she must. She'd be rude

not to. She spoons in a taste of the ember-hot congee and shuts her eyes. The emotions that flood her pull her in a thousand different directions; she has no words in any language to describe the heavy, golden feeling that settles in her chest. How can she explain what it's like, what it means, or where it comes from?

Anuya watches her. "So what news of your mother? I've not seen her in a while, what does she get up to, these days?"

Yeva's hand freezes as she's halfway to another mouthful. "I haven't seen my mother since I went to Mithrandon."

Anuya raises an eyebrow. "Oh, haven't you?"

"No. Does she still come to Daqiao often—?"

The older woman's face darkens, but only momentarily. "Oh no, she hasn't visited in years. In fact she stopped visiting Quanbao not long after you went north. A few years after, I think. I don't remember exactly. But it's been a while. She used to come round for a bowl of congee whenever she was here. And then she stopped. Why? No one can say. But I heard she and the late king had some kind of falling out. Rumors, of course. Can't say the former king was too pleased to hear her daughter had become a dragon hunter. Or so I hear."

Yeva's mouth goes dry.

Anuya scoffs; Yeva has forgotten that her face is exposed, her expressions can be read. "It's just a rumor," Anuya says. "Who knows what really happened?"

"You don't think she's—" Yeva's trying to get a thought out, *you don't think she's dead, do you?* But the words weigh down her tongue like rockfall. Clog up her throat. Only silence remains.

Anuya understands all the same. "No, no. I would have heard if something serious had happened to her. News like that would escape the village. And I still talk to my parents, you know."

Unlike me, Yeva thinks.

Anuya huffs. The mood is ruined. "Well, that's a pity. I was hoping to catch up with news from home! But I suppose there's no shortcut to it; if I want information I shall have to go pry for it myself."

Which reminds Yeva of the reason she came to town in the first place. Gingerly, she reaches for the royal seal she placed upon the table when she sat down, and pushes it forward. "This," she begins, uncertainly.

Anuya glances at it. "Yes, yes, I know," she says, almost annoyed. "Lady Sookhee will pay the tab. I wasn't going to charge you for the food, you know."

"No." Yeva taps the scale in the center of the seal. She doesn't even know why she's asking. Is it because this thing she doesn't understand is in fact a solid thing she can point to, can touch and can describe? "Tell me about this. It's dragonscale. Where did it come from?"

Anuya looks at her as if she's lost her mind. "How would

I know? Affairs of the palace are affairs of the palace, we commoners don't learn where they get their little treasures from. If only! Shouldn't you be asking the Royal Highness, not me? I'm just an old woman who sells congee."

"I'm sorry." She closes her gloved hand over the royal seal and wishes desperately to put her helmet back on. "I thought—perhaps—people would know." But it's a foolish notion. In the end, neither of them have the information the other needs. Yeva finishes the piquant meal and slowly, clumsily replaces her helmet.

Anuya says, "Even if you've grown up so far from her, you've turned out a lot more like your mother than you think. Come back anytime for a meal."

CHAPTER SIX

YEVA HAS TO wait a further two days before she's allowed to see Lady Sookhee. It's two days too long spent holed up in the orbit of her carriage, soothing Sage's anxiety, keeping her gryphons calm, suppressing bad dreams and unwanted memories that have been stirred by up her encounter with Anuya. Now's not the time to think of her family and its peculiarities, of all the secrets that her mother might have whispered to her as a child that she has forgotten, cut away as she shaped herself into the perfect weapon in service of the Sun Emperor. But she still thinks of her father as she rubs the wyrmhound behind the ears. Sage was his gift to her when she became a full-fledged knight, a pup from the best breeders in Mithrandon, big-pawed and floppy when she arrived. Her father was living elsewhere in another southern city by then. Sending Yeva to Mithrandon had destroyed her parents' union. Neither told this directly in their letters to her, but Yeva put it together from what was left unsaid. The events of that fateful afternoon when she slew that dragonling swept through all their lives like a wildfire and left only ashes behind.

On the third day, the rude handmaid Sujin returns to summon Yeva. She rakes Yeva with her gaze, tutting slightly at the sight of her metal vambraces, her heavy boots. "Still wearing that? Such an overwrought getup," she says. "Well, follow me, then. Our lady is waiting."

Yeva follows her guide toward the upper palace, climbing so many steps that even her splendid calves start to ache. What follows is a long, long walk through the incomprehensible twists of the royal compound, past rooms with screen doors muffling the hum of lively conversation; past ponds teeming with miniature terrapins and giant goldfish; past neatly raked courtyards home to swaying willows. Yeva starts off lost and gets increasingly so with every corner turned. If the handmaiden is leading her into a trap, if at the end of this twisting path she finds the slavering jaws of a dragon waiting for her, she has no means of escape. She wouldn't know the way back to her carriage, where her sacred weapon lies locked in a chest.

Lady Sookhee, the girl-king of Quentona, receives visitors in the Great Phoenix Hall, a space twice as long as it is wide, large enough to be a battlefield. Bolts of translucent cloth drape from above, rippling as the air sighs, giving the hall the fluid, ethereal appearance of an underwater palace. The steepled roof is held up by columns of wooden pillars, each taken from a single tree and paneled with intricate scenes from local legend. The craftsmanship is breathtaking. As Yeva passes by, her heart is captured by the verve in each carving, how the tiny human figures burst with motion and life, how the coiled dragons and swift deer and cloud-wreathed swallows look like they might spring from their wooden prisons at any moment.

At the end of the hall sits the throne, a heavy dais of wood and stone and brass, around which a massive serpent chiseled from the same materials rests. The dragon depicted is the southern kind, long and ropy with small, powerful limbs tipped with raptor talons, head crowned with spreading antlers. Precious gems have been pushed into each crafted scale, with rubies in the eye sockets, and their facets catch the sharp glow of the teardrop lamps purposefully hung above them. As Yeva approaches the dais, the dragon glitters and flashes as if alive.

There she is, the girl-king of Quentona—Lady Sookhee. Of similar age to Yeva, but pale and breakable as a willow branch. Not yet fully recovered from her illness, she slants upon the embroidered red cushions, knees folded and feet tucked in, head resting like a lover's against the sculpted dragon's head that peers over the seat. Around her, on raised seats only marginally less ostentatious than the throne, sit seven young women in the same peach-and-green robes as her guide. A governing council, Yeva thinks. The girl to her right has black hair so long that even the braid of it extends past her waist.

Robes of blue and pink conceal the girl-king's slender form, interrupted midway by a sash of rich indigo. The colors of a slow sunrise. The colors of the royal seal given to Yeva. Lady Sookhee's elaborately looped hair winds round a headpiece crusted with jewels and pearls, and gold bangles jingle at her wrists. She watches Yeva's approach with a hunter's intensity, a lupine intellect lurking within her fragility. Under the pressure of her attention Yeva's blood grows warm, and she's glad for the layers of metal and linen that separate her from the sight of the young monarch. She walks down the aisle as a suggestion of a human figure, an anonymous walking suit of armor, harsh and heavy in the elegance of the receiving hall.

As Sujin announces her as a knight of the Sun Empire, Yeva sinks stiffly to one knee, gaze fixed to the base of the dais. Beyond her sight, the girl-king swivels, bare feet touching ground in one fluid motion. Her toes are painted a lavender which complements the soft colors of her robes. "Thank you, Sujin," says the girl-king. "You may take your place."

"Your Majesty." Footsteps sound as Sujin joins the other women, slotting in, Yeva imagines, like a tooth.

Despite her illness, Lady Sookhee's voice is light and

clear, like rain falling upon Yeva's plumed helm. "Forgive us for leaving it so long before we were able to welcome you to our humble kingdom. It was not our intention to cause offense, but an artifact of our ill health. We do hope you have found our hospitality to be adequate in the days since your arrival."

Her Thrandish is unaccented and better articulated than Yeva's own. Yeva finally lifts her gaze and fixes it upon the girl-king. "No offense is taken. I do hope Your Majesty's health has sufficiently recovered from your illness."

"Your courtesy is appreciated." The girl-king smiles down at Yeva like a winter sun. "What a strange state of affairs this is. When the seat of the Sun Empire sends visitors, we might expect one of two things: diplomats, or an army. Yet you are neither. A single knight from the Empire's fabled guild of monster-slayers."

Yeva remains quiet. She wishes the Emperor—and Emory—had in fact sent a diplomat or an army, anyone better to carry out these fraught conversations. What does she know of speaking to kings? She is a weapon, and before that she was a peasant. Whatever skills her mother had did not transfer.

Lady Sookhee leans back in her throne, pensive. "Still, you are no ordinary knight. Your reputation precedes you. A living legend, one who songs and poems are written about—the masked guildknight of Mithrandon."

"I'm surprised such gossip has reached these borders. Your Majesty is indeed well-informed."

"Hardly." Her bright gaze seems fevered—what with, Yeva isn't sure. "Your existence has long fascinated us, even without the poetry. Your mother was a friend to the kingdom. How does the daughter of Kunlin Douma become dragonsbane, a renowned hunter of the Empire?"

Yeva is deeply glad of her conversation with Anuya days before. Through it, the revelations of her family's past and her mother's history in Quanbao have had time to settle and become architecture in her mind. Calmly and flatly she says, "It was my fate."

"A strange fate indeed. Even stranger that you should be sent to these parts years later. Tell me, daughter of Kunlin—have you, by your own will, come to find something in particular?"

Yeva ducks her head again. "I am here on the orders of my Emperor."

"Hmm." She senses the girl-king shifting in her seat, her curiosity unabated. "We cannot imagine this occurrence to simply be coincidence. Whether intended on the part of your Emperor or not."

Someone on the dais speaks to the girl-king in the language that sounds so familiar to Yeva, yet so impenetrable. It's not Sujin—this speaker sounds much younger, yet no less firm. The girl-king converses back and forth with her interlocutor while Yeva remains kneeling, feeling humiliated despite her best efforts.

"In any case, we are pleased to have an observer from the Empire in our court. We will do all we can to make your time here comfortable. And we are certain you will find suitable pursuits to occupy yourself with. We hear that you are sleeping in your carriage still. Is that so?"

"Indeed. It is my preference. My carriage is built to live in; it is where I stay when I leave Mithrandon. Within it I have devices that help me dress."

"It's no wonder, with an outfit like that. This simply will not do. You may be with us for many months—surely you cannot stay in that little carriage the whole time. You shall have a room, and some of the girls will come to move your devices in. It's fine if you wish not to have any attendants, but you must at least have a proper bed to sleep in."

She speaks as though she expects no resistance, and she shouldn't, as monarch. Yeva cannot find it in herself to refuse her orders; to do so would be to cause diplomatic offense, the one thing Emory very clearly did not want.

But the next thing she says pushes a great cold into Yeva's veins.

"Of course, we shall send you something to wear as well. You cannot be walking around in that armor all this time. Perhaps that garb might be acceptable in Mithrandon, but you are in our country now, and you should dress according to our custom. I will not have it otherwise." Her tone is more firm than it has been. The sight of the guildknight, in all that metal and leather, is offensive to her. She will not permit such things in her court.

AND SO, RELUCTANTLY, but with little recourse, Yeva is moved into the palace as the girl-king wills it. A modest room with a raised bed behind a silk screen, empty shelves, ample storage space. A view of a garden shared with neighbors. Although the room is objectively larger than Yeva's stone abode in the guildknights' fortress, it feels more oppressive somehow. One of the women from the girl-king's coterie directs servants as they move in the contents of Yeva's carriage. Yeva can only shadow them watchfully, muttering *hand of the goddess, be careful* in hopes that her tone transcends the opacity of language.

Sujin turns up to inspect their handiwork once the dust has settled. Her expression stays dour as ever, but she seems satisfied. She points down the corridor linking the rooms. "You'll find the bathhouse that way." When Yeva simply stares through her visor, she says, "Oh, yes, I forgot. You can't take off your armor around people. Well, good luck with that. The well is on the ground floor. There's a washbasin in your room for your use."

A finicky problem like this, with a single simple solution, Yeva can deal with. She fetches a basin of water, marking the path between her room and the well by decorations in courtyards and notable trees in gardens: turn here at the cherry blossom, go straight until that rock thrust up like a closed fist. She undresses, cleans herself, and gets ready to dress again.

As a matter of courtesy, the girl-king has sent her several sets of clothing of the style worn in Quanbao. Wraparound trousers and a simple inner tunic to be pulled over the head, long-sleeved liner robes and outer robes all tied closed with sashes, and something like a surcoat to go over it, but tied in front. All in plain and hard-wearing materials, something like a servant might don. Yeva cannot decide if this is a courtesy or an insult—she cannot put on the elaborate getups of the palace ladies without aid, but should she want to? She runs her hands over the coarse weave of the fabric and thinks, what would I be wearing now if I hadn't gone to Mithrandon? The trappings of her knight's outfit feel too cumbersome for her delicate environs: the dragonscale, the steel boots.

Hesitant, Yeva picks out a set in shades of gray and deep blue. She's not sure if she'll like it, if the color will suit her. Since she went to Mithrandon, she has not had to choose what to wear, and all understanding of fashion has fled from her mind. The experience is excruciatingly novel. But the robes provided go on easily, even with her maimed hand. They sit light on her shoulders, so gentle she feels like she might float into the air, untethered by the pull of the earth. The sleeves go to her wrist, loose enough she can tuck her hands in them if needed, but really they are no protection at all, showing brown skin untouched by the sun, the clawlike appendage riven with scars. The monarch has even provided Yeva with matching socks and soft-soled slippers. This is no soldier's outfit; no article will bear the touch of a dagger or the violent pull of a claw.

Now all that's missing is a head covering, and of course, one is not provided. Yeva may concede a lot to the girl-king's wishes, but this is the only thing she cannot be persuaded from. The thought of walking about with her face open to the elements is unbearable; the one incident in the congee restaurant has taught her never to do it again. Yeva completes her outfit by donning her plumed helm of shining metal—and feels an instant wave of shame. The incongruity of the Empire's heavyweight handiwork made even more obtrusive. Is she to spend all her days in Daqiao looking like this, feeling like this?

Someone at the door: Sujin, returning to tell her that the girl-king seeks a private audience. Yeva cannot refuse and there's no time to change back into her usual garb. Dressed like a fool, she sheepishly trails after Sujin. Even with the weight of her helm pressing upon her head, she still feels like she might trip over her feet and fall into the sky. The handmaiden says nothing of Yeva's mismatched outfit.

A long climb: the girl-king's private quarters are tucked within the highest floors of the palace. Behind doors screened with paper so thick it seems like cotton, a vast room of ebony and rosewood sprawls in decadence. Sandalwood and cedar burn in incense dishes. Intricate tasseled lanterns hang from the rafters by the hundreds, some the size of a human child, some small enough to fit her palm. A beautiful writing desk sits at one end, appointed with paper and ink, surrounded by shelves of bound volumes. On the other, bedchambers obscured by more paper screens painted with emblems of the royal seal, dragons, and lotuses.

The room's beating heart is a long, low tea table with attendant lounging chairs, upon which the monarch of Quanbao stretches. Her coterie orbits her, making her comfortable, chattering in their shared language. One of them—the girl with long braided hair—kneels at the table and crumbles herbs into a glass pot bubbling over a tea light. When Yeva enters, amusement titters through the pack of them. Lady Sookhee covers her mouth as she smiles. "I'm glad my gift appears to your liking," she says. "Although your choice of headgear leaves much to be desired, as usual."

The long-haired girl, eyes bright and sharp, makes an

observation. Yeva thinks she catches a syllable like the word for "broth" in her home language.

Lady Sookhee laughs; for someone so frail, her laughter bursts like a firework, thunderous and golden. "Kima says you look like a soup ladle. All skinny, with a big round metal head."

Amusement sweeps the room. Yeva catches sight of herself in a bronze mirror; the handmaiden isn't wrong. She does look like a kitchen implement. More importantly, she understood the word *soup*. There's bleed between their languages. Hope soars within her: with time and directed effort, she might be able to understand it.

"Sujin," the girl-king begins, then continues in her tantalizing language, a series of instructions. The grumpy maid vanishes briefly and returns with an elaborately lacquered black box. On its lid, painted in golds and reds, a sinuous dragon wraps a cloud-wreathed moon.

Lady Sookhee gently places it beside her and nods to dismiss her servants. The others leave without a fuss, but Sujin has parting advice for Yeva: "You'd better behave yourself, Soup Ladle."

Alone now, Lady Sookhee laughs. "Please pardon my council. They're usually fairly well-behaved, decorous as could be, but sometimes they can't help a little mischief. They mean nothing by it."

"I don't mind."

A broad gesture to the other lounge chair. "Please, have a seat."

She does, perching on the edge of the sleek fabric in her new robes to study the creature before her in close quarters. Lady Sookhee seems to have shed the coat of ice she wore earlier, less monarch and more young woman, not all that different from Yeva. Only that Yeva is busy being a soup ladle, apparently. The golden brew in the pot draws her gaze: she recognizes its color and aroma. "Is that five-leaf warming tea?"

"Your senses are sharp. It is indeed. It helps with my blood disease. But you know what it does, of course. After all, it was your mother who taught mine about the effects of this tea. She was very knowledgeable about afflictions of the body."

"She made this tea for you?"

"For my mother, mostly. I inherited her condition; it runs in our bloodline. Unfortunate, but it is what it is. I have learned to accept the limitations of my body."

Yeva nods. With her maimed hand she carefully works at the bubbling teapot, turning the metal stick in looped circles the way her mother taught her, managing the delicate movements by stirring from the wrist.

She says: "I've not seen my mother since I went to Mithrandon a dozen years ago. You probably know her better than I."

Lady Sookhee laughs. "I hardly knew her! She was my mother's friend, not mine. They would find excuses to be alone and away from me. And she hasn't come to Quanbao in a dozen years. Not even for my mother's wake. They had some kind of quarrel around the time of my royal father's death; she stopped visiting not too long after."

"Your father's death?" Now this is new to Yeva. There are no tales of the men who married the kings of Quanbao, none that she knows of, neither story nor fact. Their glaring absence has long been part of the kingdom's mysteries.

"Ah. Matters of a time long past. Let's not speak of them." Lady Sookhee smiles coyly, as if she has said too much. Her gentle hands stop Yeva's stirring so she can pour the brew into a clear glass cup. That brief instance of contact, cool skin against skin, startles the thoughts out of Yeva's mind.

Lady Sookhee sips her tea with deerlike grace. "Forgive me for how coldly I spoke earlier. I wasn't sure about you, given your reputation. The Sun Emperor wraps his ambition in beautiful wreaths of friendship, and when the envoy sent to us is not a man of letters but an armed and dangerous knight, one has to be cautious. But you don't seem like a strident planter of banners, someone come to brand the Empire's marks upon our flanks." She puts the cup down. "I asked if you had come to Quanbao looking for something.

That was my personal curiosity. I wondered if perhaps you were looking for traces of what your mother learned in this country."

Beneath her helm, Yeva licks her dry lips and swallows. The truth is easiest to let out: "I never chose to come. That was my guildmaster's decision—the Emperor did not order this either. He wanted to send a whole company of men instead. With their servants all told, it would have been a party of nearly a hundred."

"I see." Lady Sookhee looks thoughtful. "So truly no one wished you here. And yet you have come. It's almost like there are greater forces at work...."

Yeva holds her breath for two counts, steadying herself. A question burns the back of her throat and she must let it out. "The royal seal you gave me," she begins. "It's dragonscale. Is it not?"

"An observation as sharp as expected of a guildknight of Mithrandon. It is indeed. Dragonscale is an extremely rare material, as you well know. What you have is a precious relic of our nation, only given to dignitaries and those we want to honor. Please take good care of it."

Yeva entwines her hands in her lap to keep them still. "What I have to ask next will be awkward. But I must ask it. His Radiance believes that Quentona—that Quanbao is home to a dragon that eluded our grasp years ago. Is that true? Do you harbor such creatures?"

The girl-king laughs her firework laugh until a cough takes hold of her. On some unknown instinct Yeva jumps up to attend to her, kneeling by her side, reaching out to rub her back.

Lady Sookhee pushes her hand away. "Forgive me. My health is not..." The moment of vulnerability passes and she straightens up, once more the unflappable monarch. She smiles. "I understand your question and why you ask it. Dragons are sacred to us, they form the basis of our culture. But if you're asking about the sort of beasts you hunt, then—no. They do not live here. Not anymore."

For a brief moment sadness envelops her like a flash of ice. But before Yeva can latch on to it, Lady Sookhee puts it aside and returns a small smile to her face. But this gesture of reticence only endears her to Yeva, who has spent a lifetime putting her own emotions into neat boxes where they won't bother others.

Lady Sookhee picks up the lacquered box beside her. "I have a gift for you. Consider it an apology for my behavior earlier."

Still kneeling, Yeva accepts the box and hinges it open. Within it, a wooden half-mask sits upon a cushion of velvety fabric. A dragon mask, painted in red and gold, its workmanship exquisite, jewels set into the ends of its faux horns. Yeva gingerly lifts it into the light. Her pulse quickens for reasons she cannot articulate.

Lady Sookhee says: "This mask used to be your mother's."

Words fail her. She glances at the girl-king with a trembling gaze the other can't see.

She continues: "Once, many years ago—before either of us were born—your mother spent the spring festival in Daqiao. She took part in the Festival of Return, where we all don masks for a night and mingle, everyone from every walk of life. This was the one she chose. My mother kept it in her room, it was precious to her. I thought it might suit you. After all, it must be difficult to eat and drink in that metal bucket of yours."

Yeva runs her thumbs over the polished, painted wood. The mask smells of sandalwood, of the box it was kept in. Still, its paint shines, unsullied and wax-fresh. Worn once and kept in the dark, a precious jewel. She imagines her mother with this mask over her face, draped in golden robes and locked arm-in-arm with the young girl-king of a bygone age, pretending to be a pair of commoners eating sweets at a festival market. A beautiful, romantic image that fills her head with foolish light. Abstract figures that capture her heart nonetheless.

"You can try it on to see if you like it," Lady Sookhee says. "I'll turn around. I promise I won't look."

How can Yeva refuse? Each step into Quanbao has seen the breaking of one taboo after another. She removed her helm for Anuya. She has shed the vestments of the guild for a stranger's robes. What does it matter, swapping her cumbersome metal helm for this sleek, fearless mask? She turns her body away from Lady Sookhee to make the switch, but part of her wants to do it without decorum, to expose the lines of her face to the girl-king and absorb all the consequences.

The sandalwood scent of the mask enfolds her like a pair of gentle arms, warm and inviting. The world feels much lighter, its colors sharper. Open air breathes softly upon the nape of her neck. Almost shyly, Yeva meets Lady Sookhee's gaze again, and finds herself graced by a tiny half-moon of a smile. "You look wonderful."

She ducks her head in a nod. The mask hides her eyes but not her mouth; if she frowns it will be seen, if she struggles to find her way around a word it will be witnessed. It feels like part of her has cracked, but in the way frost cracks in the spring.

"Thank you," she says, softly, in the language of home.

Lady Sookhee straightens up, attentive. "*Thank you,*" she says, but in her own native tongue, and Yeva understands it. The syllables are all different, but she recognizes each one in the language she already knows. All of a sudden the wall of understanding between them seems not so insurmountable. All of a sudden the woman in front of her is not the monarch of an unfriendly nation, but someone she could be friends with. Someone she could let into the chambers of her heart.

The girl-king says, "We don't know how long you will be with us. But while you're here, let us make the most of it. Perhaps you will find something worthy of your time during your stay."

CHAPTER SEVEN

THUS BEGAN THE masked guildknight's long stay in Daqiao. Outside of Mithrandon's walls, in absence of marching orders and the routines she had followed for so many years, Kunlin Yeva discovers the joy and burdens of freedom. The time to do what she wants and the impossibility of deciding what that should be. She can only carry out so many weapon drills. Made tender by nostalgia, she allows the delights offered by this new country to creep into her heart and unfurl like the white petals of a peony. Within the labyrinthine layout of the royal palace she discovers little pleasures: wisteria gardens dripping with spring blossoms, stately libraries whose heavy air lies still as the mountains, steam-clad hot-spring baths which she slips into when she finds herself alone. She accepts Captain Lu's invitations to dinners, where she discovers the breadth and depth of local cuisine in the company of his rowdy lieutenants. She wanders into town not as a marauder but as a guest, bringing the royal seal with her as a mark of favor, allowing her to go wherever she pleases.

The world looks, feels, tastes different in her new light garb. After years of wading through the world in armor, the robes seem gauzy despite their weight and thickness, as if she were wrapped in spider silk. In dress she seems not so different from the merchants and the children shrieking as they race around in courtyards, limbs flailing. Her half-mask allows her to feel the air on her lips, to taste soft floured snacks when they're offered to her, to smile in gratitude when she feels it.

But a soldier taken from the barracks is still a soldier by habit, and Yeva struggles to feel complete without a duty to perform. Tasked to investigate if Quanbao might harbor secret dragons, she finds herself caught by the possibility of any clue wherever she goes—certain sounds or stories turning her head, a flash of cream-white like dragonbone prompting a question of—*what's that made of?* Anything that is secret or legendary or hidden catches her interest.

Eventually, one of Captain Lu's men—a loose-lipped hothead named Chuwan—lets slip that the massive cave system that hollows the mountains around them also runs deep in the bedrock under the palace. "Caves? No one's mentioned any," Yeva says, intrigued. "Tell me more."

"Oh," Chuwan says quickly, "it's nothing at all. Just some old caves. You shouldn't go anyway, it's off-limits. There's lava and whatnot in there."

This only serves to make Yeva's curiosity worse. She brings it up to Lady Sookhee that evening. "Tell me about the caves at the castle."

The girl-king giggles and gently corrects: "You mean *around* the castle. Or underneath." She's been teaching Yeva her language, at Yeva's request. Every evening they spend curled up in her lantern-draped chambers, speaking of infinitives and gerunds. Vocabulary comes easy to Yeva but grammar is hard. Prepositions the worst of all. Lady Sookhee asks: "Why are you interested in the caves?"

Yeva sieves through her meager pool of words to put a sentence together. "I want to study them. If there's something interesting in them, I want to see."

Her eyes crinkle in amusement at Yeva's struggle. "You can speak Thrandish if it's easier."

It would be easier, but Yeva knows she won't improve if she keeps taking the easy way out. She stubbornly continues in her new language. "I would like to see them. Even if it's dangerous."

"Hmm." Lady Sookhee taps her chin. "I would not normally grant permission, and there are times when the caves are closed to everyone, even members of the royal family. Did you understand that? It would be forbidden—this word you know. But it isn't right now, and if you're so curious..." She leans forward, her hands on her knees. "Come. I will give you instructions. This should strengthen your understanding of directions. I'd like to see how you navigate those caves on your own."

That's how Yeva finds herself tiptoeing through the lower levels of the palace with Sage at her heels, carefully separating the words for *left* and *right*, repeating the girl-king's words over and over until she finds the correct place in the correct library, the one filled with foreign books from the world over. One specific rosewood shelf with an indent whose shape she recognizes well, which accepts the royal seal of dragonscale. The whole bookshelf draws aside to reveal bedrock, rough-hewn stairs tumbling into the bones of the earth. Yeva, wielding a torch, descends into the cool dark, into vast chambers of glossy black rock echoing with the faint sound of water. For the first time since she had come to Daqiao, she has put her armor back on, and the weight settles back onto her bones with such ease she almost resents it. Resents the speed at which her gait adjusts to the stiffness of what she wears. Yet the familiarity is comforting, like an old bed well slept in. With the flickering torch held aloft she feels once again like a faceless soldier, as she has been for the bulk of her life. Sage lopes ahead of her, sniffing the ground for danger, pointing the way forward. She takes mental notes as a soldier would, charting the intestinal rope of the path she takes between these great hollows, as though planning for an invasion, as though seeking out spots an enemy could hide. She is on alert, scanning the environment with all her senses, even though she has no reason to suspect she might be in peril. It is an old, exhausting habit, this paranoia of hers.

An entire world seems to languish in this unknown dark. Yeva's mind plays tricks on her, conjuring images of massive otherworldly shapes moving through the caves alongside her watching her passage with glittering red eyes. Still her sacred blood remains quiet under her skin, telling her that nothing draconic lives in these caves. If something dangerous were hiding in these passages, she would know.

Yeva keeps walking, one heavy foot in front of the next, until the air grows unbearably warm, until the bluish light from the lichen sticking to the walls is superseded by a hellish glow. She's found the lava pools, red molten rock welling up from deep underground, so bright and hot in their excess that even Yeva, who makes her keep slaying beasts of nightmare, cannot bear to be around them. She makes a note in her mind: a dead end.

Later that evening Lady Sookhee asks: "Did you find anything in your journey through the caves?"

"They're very big," she says. "And hotter than I expected."

She nods, seeming pleased by Yeva's answer. "They're not safe to explore; they're sealed off for a reason. I have to protect my subjects; people often have more curiosity than they have sense. But since you are a knight, I let you go. If there was any trouble, I thought you could handle it."

Yeva agrees. "They were no problem."

Thus these halcyon days go on, so golden and even-keeled that they might go on forever. Yeva becomes a regular at the stalls of Daqiao's market streets. She becomes proficient enough in the local tongue to make small talk, ask after children, laugh at jokes. They call her Soup Ladle and Bucket Head still, and she lets them—it's funny. The palace guards, her dining companions, become comrades whose temperaments and dislikes she understands better than the guildknights' she served with for years. Bit by bit she stops looking for clues of a dragon infestation. Bit by bit she forgets why she was sent here.

One day Aunty Anuya asks, "You've been here a few months, have you thought of going home for a visit?"

Yeva has come by for tea and snacks, a weekly affair she has worked into her schedule of work, learning, and leisure. The question catches her off guard: her first thought being *Why? I don't miss Mithrandon,* until she understands what Aunty Anuya is really asking. Struck by sudden panic like a musket shot to the chest, she counters with a question of her own. "When was the last time *you* went home for a visit?" And as Aunty Anuya laughs and capitulates—"Choy, choy, who's going to run the shop if I leave?"—she is spared from having to give a solid answer, spared from having to pry open the lid of her chest and look inside at the tangled, bloody mess that is her thoughts about home and mother.

She has actively cut that section of her life away, and the resulting wound she does not want to think about.

Weeks pass. Months pass. It's the longest stretch of time since Yeva has been on a hunt, and yet she doesn't feel idle. She writes to Emory, sending falcons to and fro, bearing two documents each time: an official report, dry as old bone, and a personal letter full of the life and color on the streets of Daqiao. She continues to explore the caves beneath the royal palace, sketching out detailed maps of their intricate chambers and lava roadblocks. She's not always allowed: for stretches of weeks at a time the caves are too dangerous to enter and guards are posted in front of its secret entrance. In those days, Yeva waits impatiently to be allowed passage again. Down in the dark, with nothing but air between her and the raging firmament, she feels shockingly small and blessedly mortal, both awed by the scale and enervated by a sense of discovery. It reminds her of a particular child a long time ago, creeping through a swamp and limestone cave with her little sister, hand in clammy hand, giggling at every strange fungus they discover, at every striped newt that scuttles away from them. A memory so long buried it has nearly decayed into the dirt. Freshly unearthed, parts of it still glisten.

Finally there's Lady Sookhee. The girl-king of Quanbao treats her with such warmth and gentleness Yeva does not know what to do with herself. Some days a single smile from the monarch sets her heart racing, and such dizziness sweeps through her she has to remain absolutely still lest she lose her balance and fall. When they are in the same room, Yeva teeters between joy and anxiety, admiration and loathing, and she cannot explain the tides of emotion that swell and retreat within her. When they are apart, Yeva's thoughts often stray to the girl-king: what would she say or do at this moment, what should Yeva do that might amuse her? And when she falls ill—as she does with alarming regularity, every month, like clockwork—Yeva finds herself pacing the walkways of the palace as she is denied access to its monarch. She is not used to attaching emotion to people she knows, and this novel experience is as uncomfortable as it is pleasurable.

The spring of the year brings new hopes, new promises, new experiences. Daqiao shrugs off the blanket of winter with an eruption of sounds and light and joy. In Yeva's childhood, spring festivals were glazed with the steam of hotpot around a table, the light of a fire in the garden, windows decorated with paper cutouts. In the royal palace, servants festoon branches with red ribbons and put up strings of paper lanterns. The corridors bustle as they rush to and fro with their arms full of sweets, baskets of fruit, bundles of cloth, decorative scrolls, lacquered boxes, cooking supplies, cleaning supplies, bamboo baskets, gardening tools. In town, the buildings blossom into explosions of color. Paper lanterns hang in strings, bright as songbirds, and every window trails streamers and wind-catchers. Activity builds up to a crescendo as the Festival of Return approaches, the apex of the spring festival in Quanbao. The same festival which Lady Sookhee spoke of, attended by Yeva's mother years ago.

The girl-king summons Yeva to her chambers on the eve of the festival. One of her lounge chairs holds a matching set of elaborate blue robes trimmed in gold. Upon the indigo folds of one sits another painted dragon half-mask, this one in shades of green and black. The girl-king smiles as understanding dawns on Yeva. "It's the Festival of Return tonight. And as is tradition, as my mother did before me, I will don a mask and walk among the people, and they will be none the wiser. There's a market, music, performances. Yeva, will you accompany me? So that I need not walk alone."

"Do you always go alone?"

"No. I'll usually have one of my girls with me, of course. Or a few. But this year, since you're here—I'd like it to be you."

"People already recognize me by my mask," Yeva says. "They'll know it's me, and then they'll realize it's you."

Lady Sookhee smiles, brilliant and pale as a pearl. "That's fine. Will you?"

How could she refuse? It's how the pair of them, fluid in their disguises, leap into a world bursting with song and flavor. Down through the market they go, speeding over the shining cobblestones, Yeva tugged along by Lady Sookhee. The girl-king seems entirely at ease in her masked anonymity, much like Yeva herself. This fact brings Yeva an unusual happiness, a kind of relief. Warmth spreads from her chest into her limbs, and she feels so light that gravity might lose its grip on her and allow her to fly into the endless winds of the night.

The two slip between exuberant bodies, elbowing their way to the front of stalls, finding pockets of air to grin at each other, tucking themselves into small spaces of calm under the eaves of buildings to wolf down the snacks they bought. Lady Sookhee tries a bit of everything: roasted nuts in cones of paper, bags of every fruit preserve, grilled meats on sticks, balls of fried dough, sticky rice cake filled with lotus paste or bean paste or groundnuts. There are stalls which sell lanterns, and little wooden toys for children, and inflatable balls made of colored paper; stalls which offer bushels of flowers and beautifully sculpted hairpins and chrysanthemums the size of a child's head. She buys a sandalwood fan with legends of dragons carved through the thin slats, each panel no bigger than a thumbnail, and slips it into Yeva's sleeve pocket.

The clamor increases. It's time for the dragon dance. Bodies pack the main thoroughfare so densely it's impassable. Wedged in the crowd, they might not get to see anything. "Come," Yeva says. She leads Lady Sookhee away from the crowd and slips into Aunty Anuya's teahouse. "Let us use your second-floor balcony," she entreats.

On the mezzanine the air is finally cool again. Lady Sookhee leans over the parapet as down below the troupe begins their performance. The dragon, propped on metal rods, made of yards of shimmering fabric lined with the black fur of goats, undulates over the heads of twenty dancers in bright red outfits. Cymbals clash and trumpets blare as the dancers twirl the dragon's ropy body into flowing shapes like a river. Lady Sookhee watches the dance with a soft joy that almost looks like melancholy. "Has anyone told you the meaning behind this dance? Behind the Festival of Return?"

"Tell me."

A smile, a fond look at the dancing below. As the thunder and song of performance clangs around them, she spins her tale. "The Spring Festival celebrates the return of the children of Chuan-pu, the ancestral dragon. It is said that our forebears first came to Quanbao when it was but a wild land, hostile mountains that bore no trees and shook with the anger of the gods. They had fled a terrible war and were hungry and weak. The eldest daughter of their leader was a girl of twenty named Suma, and she was tougher than the mountains and prettier than the meadows in spring. As Chuan-pu circled the heavens, he saw her hunting in the river to feed her family, and his heart was instantly captured by her beauty, her resilience. He came down to the mortal world in the shape of a man to court her, to woo her. At first, she was not interested in something so banal as a human boy. But when he revealed his godly nature, her heart was swayed. They fell in love. Suma kept him company at night, and he used his magic to help the refugees settle into this harsh land. He married Suma, and she bore him many children, half-human and half-dragon.

"But still they suffered. The mountains were not kind to our forebears. Harvests were meager and winters harsh. Children starved and infants died in their cribs. Seeing the pain suffered by Suma's people, Chuan-pu was so moved by sorrow that he decided to offer up the thing most precious to him: his life. He sacrificed himself and became part of the land, his flesh nourishing the soil and his bones calming the tremors of the earth. His divine essence turned a wasteland into a blessed paradise, and from then on Quanbao flourished."

They've slipped back to Thrandish without Yeva even noticing. "So this dance is to honor Chuan-pu's sacrifice?"

"Mm. Partly. The dance is also known as *The Dragon's Return*. According to legend, the children of Chuan-pu, who themselves are half-draconic, would assume their sacred forms and wander the world and spirit realms for half a year, during which the kingdom of Quanbao would grow cold and its ground hard."

"Ah. So an allegory for winter, then."

"Precisely. The return of the dragons signifies the return of warm weather, the return of the sun and the return of shoots budding through tender loam."

"How poetic of you," Yeva murmurs, earning her an elbow in the ribs. Below them, the dance reaches its climax, the silk dragon spinning in huge spirals as the music grows joyous and frenetic. How little these spiritual beasts of legend resemble the reptilian creatures of blood and bone Yeva has hunted all her life. The Sun Emperor is a fool to think that they are anything alike.

Lady Sookhee complains of exhaustion after the festivities. They retire to the palace, where the sound of firecrackers and celebration becomes a soft, hazy backdrop. "I shall take a bath," the girl-king declares. "Will you join me?"

Blood rushes through Yeva's body; exposed to the air, her cheeks and ears burn. Two warring versions of her appear at that moment: one that cleaves to sanity and propriety, to whom the obvious answer is to refuse as a knight and envoy should. The other wants to give in, to say yes, to see where this will lead. She's sure she knows where it will lead, but she's too afraid to admit it.

"Come," Lady Sookhee says, a gentle entreaty, and she takes Yeva's scarred hand with such tenderness that whatever objections she had collapse, folding under the weight of Yeva's desires.

The girl-king leads her into the fragrant quiet of her private garden, which Yeva has not yet been within. It's larger than she knew: a courtyard of raked stone, a trellis knotted with herbs, slim benches for moon-gazing. At its furthest end, citrus bushes and rock sculptures surround a hot spring from which rosettes of steam billow. They undress and slide into the warm fog. Beneath the rilling water and a thin layer of steam, the pale shape of Lady Sookhee's body is so long and narrow she appears to be half-serpent, smooth and limbless, all muscle that could coil around a waist or a throat, snapping bone as it went. An old scar runs down the side of her ribs, and Yeva, out of curiosity, reaches to touch it, to run her finger down its crooked line, only pulling back at the last second.

Sookhee laughs. "Are you shy, guildknight?"

"I'm not," Yeva says, acutely defensive. Still, she stumbles over her words. "It's just..."

Sookhee takes Yeva's unmasked face in her hands and studies it, thumbs sliding across her cheekbones. Yeva finds her mind going blank, thoughts of duty and the world outside slipping away like rainwater. The girl-king has finally broken through the last of the barriers she had built around herself. At this moment, at this twilight, she is allowed to take on new form—not just the valiant guildknight of the Sun Empire, not the faithful servant whose only purpose is to wield a blade, not the faceless, nameless creature who exists only as terror and whispered legend. She never lets herself be so exposed, yet she does not feel vulnerable. She leans into the girl-king as the young woman pulls around her. She sheds her reservations. Later, when they retire to her bedchambers, she allows herself to sigh, to linger in sensations, to wrap her fingers in the damp ribbons of Lady Sookhee's hair. Her lover licks the salt from her navel, travels with her fingers between Yeva's legs, and when she moans *yes, please, yes,* the words that slide from her lips emerge in the language of home, sounds and syllables she has been divorced from for so long.

In the clear, quiet aftermath, Lady Sookhee says, "I'm glad you came to us," as she drums fingers against Yeva's clavicle. The bones of her ankle rest against Yeva's foot, and Yeva can feel the pulse in their bellies pressed together. "Selfish as it is, I wish you'd stay longer with us. Perhaps for good, even."

Yeva's stomach lurches as if rolling off a great cliff at the thought of abandoning Mithrandon and the life she has known thus far. She can't conceptualize it; she would never have thought of such a thing herself. She has no answer to that, nothing to say to such a crazy fantasy. She shuts her eyes and buries her face in the crook of Sookhee's arm, as though it might substitute for putting her armor on again.

CHAPTER EIGHT

WEEKS AFTER THE spring festival, Lady Sookhee's blood-illness returns for its usual rounds. Yeva is again left alone to her own devices. Now that they have become lovers, she feels the absence of the girl-king even more than usual, like the empty socket of a tooth, like a limb cut off. At the same time, a wave of stomach ailments sweeps the ranks of the palace guards, leaving her even less to distract herself with.

On the third day of Lady Sookhee's seclusion, Captain Lu summons her. "Look. You know my men are down for the count. We're short-staffed. I want you to guard the door in the library—you know the one."

The door, the secret door that leads to the caverns that are once again barred to the world. Yeva agrees, even though the request is ludicrous and they both know it—she is an Imperial guest, and not someone to be ordered around like a pantry maid. And yet she likes the tacit acknowledgment that she's become almost like household staff. Yeva takes the wyrmhound Sage with her and stands guard in the stillness of the library with the knowledge of the secret entrance that waits behind her. She's dressed herself in her guildknight's armor again, old habit—if she is to do a soldier's duty, then a soldier's garb she must don. Varuhelt, her sacred weapon, idle since she came here, sits at her waist, waiting to be useful. It feels only proper.

No one comes to the library, of course. These books serve as an archive and are rarely read; even the palace scholars haunt these shelves fleetingly, just visiting to look up a specific volume before vanishing again. None would come to try the secret entrance to the caverns. It was only ever Yeva who bothered the guards, asking, "Still closed today, is it? I'll come again tomorrow, then."

Now she's the one watching over that forbidden entrance. Sage sits beside her to keep her company, infinitely patient in a way Yeva is not. The unoccupied hours yawn before her, a guildknight trained for battle and not for standing guard. The idle wheels of her mind spin in place. She thinks, and she's been thinking, that there's a pattern to the regularity of these two phenomena, the unrest in the caverns and Lady Sookhee's illness. Don't they always overlap? Doesn't the girl-king always fall ill when some unknown calamity is striking the heart of the caverns, making it too dangerous for human passage? What if the threat that lurks within these deep hells is the same thing that plagues Lady Sookhee, the fumes of its miasma coming through the stone and creeping into the royal bedchambers as her lover sleeps? The thought, once kindled in her head, continues to burn and burn until it is a wall of flame that blots out any other rational thought. The thought of those deep caverns with their immense size and unexplained dangers gains form and mass until she can feel it pressing down on the back of her neck. She cannot turn away from these feelings; she's trapped by them. That sense of suffocation sharpens Yeva's instincts for danger, raising the temperature of her blood until she knows she must act. She is a guildknight of Mithrandon; she cannot simply stand idle.

So it is that Yeva turns and activates the secret doorway she is meant to be safeguarding. So it is that she descends the stairway she was supposed to protect from access.

She's not sure what she's expecting to find. Her weeks of exploration have made familiar ground of the hostile subterranean landscape, but the purported dangers that cause it to be sealed away have never been explained to her. Neither has she found clues in the before and after. But she's only been at this for a handful of months; there's things she could have missed. Yeva's heart races at the thought of what she might find, but she is used to living this way. Used to feeling alive this way.

The cool dark of the caverns seems the same as she left it. Nothing gives way under her feet. Nothing leaps out at her from the shadows. No fumes clog the air; nothing burns her lungs as she breathes. Yeva holds her torch aloft and walks through unchanged terrain, wondering what she might be missing. And yet her blood, her sacred blood, squirms in her veins as anxieties skitter over her skin. That particular sense of hers has been quiet since she came to Quanbao, lulling her into a false sense of calm. Now, her instincts are on full alert. The bones of her arm ache, as though responding to a threat.

Something lurks within these chambers that wasn't here before.

Sage sniffs the air and grumbles, ears laid back. The wyrmhound falls in step with her master as they press onward. Yeva tracks her growing sense of unease, letting its volume guide her through the caverns as though following Sage's keen nose. Whatever they're following leaves neither physical scent nor trail; it might be of supernatural nature. A demon that curses these lands.

Much as Yeva dreads, she is led toward lava. In the crimson furnace of a hollow groaning and popping with magma she comes to a stop, unable to proceed further. The source of her unease lies beyond these walls, and she cannot reach it. She sweats in her helm, suddenly and keenly aware of its discomfort. It seems she will have to turn back, with nothing to show for her transgressions.

Sage goes stiff in alert, ears pricked as she points to something Yeva has missed. Following the sulfurous curve of the lava leads her to the edge of the cavern. A fracture in its hard glossy walls, almost invisible in the hellish light. Has it always been here, has she simply missed its existence in all her exploring, or was it opened up by whatever she's hunting? Not that it matters. The gap is large enough for someone to walk through it, and walk through she does, into a darkness that grows colder and quieter as she leaves the magma fissure behind.

The crack in the rock widens the further she goes until it's almost a decent passageway, and the movement of air around her hints at a larger volume waiting ahead. What is there? This is uncharted territory; in her months of exploring she has never made it past the lava barrier. Whatever secrets the caverns have been hiding, she is about to find out.

At last the passageway ends and before her is a cavern that dwarfs any other she's mapped in her expeditions underground. She stands on a ledge that overlooks a new world enclosed within the belly of the earth. It's so large she cannot see the other end; it's so large that she can hear a river rushing in the distance, the muffled roar of a waterfall. It's so large she can imagine a city planted here and growing, hidden from the eyes of goddess and emperor. Her feeble torch throws a meager circle of light that barely illuminates a fraction of what she's discovered. A sky-blue glow runs like lightning across the ground and collects in outcroppings of rock that thrust upward like stalagmites. Firefly freckles of holy phosphorescence, not unlike the glow of her sacred weapon when she activates it. Exactly like that glow, in fact.

Yeva can barely breathe and she feels dizzy. She gestures for Sage to reconnoiter and the eager wyrmhound leaps off the ledge with brindled wings spread, soaring through the yawning cavern in search of lurking danger. She watches Sage tilt into the shadows until she is a pinprick, too faint to distinguish in the gloom. A whistle recalls her faithful companion, who lands in a flurry of fur and feathers and bumps her nose into Yeva's waiting hand.

Sage has found nothing, but it doesn't mean it's safe. Carefully, Yeva climbs down from the ledge, torch held aloft in her maimed hand. There's something she must investigate. Gingerly, she approaches the closest glowing outcrop. As its light pulses, the blood in her veins throbs in concert. She presses the palm of her broken hand upon the rock and shivers as the blue fire within her, the ability she spent her youth carefully cultivating, bursts into instant recognition. This is the same material that forms the core of her holy weapon, Varuhelt—it forms the core of all sacred weapons in the Empire, in fact. This, the rarest of rare materials, thought to be found only in the most blessed of locations touched by the sun, yet it languishes here in such vast quantities underground. All this time while Yeva explored the bright colors and sweet gardens of Daqiao above, a whole second world has lurked under her feet. Yeva walks from bright stone to bright stone, eyes awash with wonder, mind reeling with the implications of her discovery.

And then she sees it: a wide swathe of scale glittering upon the floor, appearing like a scatter of cherry blossoms at first, iridescent in the crosshatch of her torch and the holy blue light. Her heart leaps into her mouth as she realizes what she's looking at. She picks a single specimen off the floor and flexes it: still soft, not yet stiffened into the indomitable material that makes the prized armor she wears. Fresh dragon shed, no more than a day or two old.

A dragon has been here, in this cavern, not too long ago—a living creature, one still growing and breathing. There can be no other explanation.

A constellation of fears explodes within Yeva. A hundred different thoughts and a thousand different questions all at once. She has been lied to. She has been told the wrong version of the truth. She's discovered something everyone knew. She's discovered something nobody knew.

A dragon lives in Quanbao, making its nest somewhere deep in the mountains protecting its capital city. The Emperor was right. She was not sent to this kingdom on an idle whim.

Yeva wants to chase after this beast. She wants a hundred questions answered. She wants to begin the hunt. She wants to return to the palace to shake Lady Sookhee and ask—did you know? Is this why the caverns are sealed off? Have you been lying to me, even as we shared a bed, shared our hearts?

Her fingers close around the still-living scale, blotting out its soft iridescence. She knows what her next steps are. Her need for answers wins. To plunge deeper into alien territory in pursuit of unknown quarry would be foolishness. Her hunt is only beginning.

As Yeva retraces her footsteps a great heat builds in her chest and continues swelling as she approaches the surface. By the time she emerges into the bright, cold light of the royal palace she feels ready to burst into flame. Without speaking to anyone else, she heads directly to Lady Sookhee's bedchambers, one broad step after another, walking so quick even Sage has to trot to keep up.

Her way is barred—the grumpy handmaiden Sujin stands guard before a palisade of embroidered screens that stretches across the walkway. Over the months Sujin has softened toward her, but among Lady Sookhee's personal staff she has softened the least, keeping one watchful eye upon this intrusion in her mistress's inner circle. Yeva is denied access in the most tight-lipped, uninterested way: you can't go further. Those are the rules.

"This is important," she insists. "A matter of Daqiao's safety. The city is in danger."

Unimpressed, Sujin flicks her gaze toward the sky in

the central courtyard. "Is the city on fire? Is it burning down? Are the Emperor's troops at the gates, about to break through it?"

"No, but—"

"Then it can wait two days."

"This is—"

"I said, it can wait two days."

Yeva has gotten so comfortable that she's forgotten her place in this country: a guest who has no say in what the girl-king must do. She is an outsider who cannot choose to do as she pleases. Foolishly, she had thought differently. Fuming, full of resentment, she retreats to the room she was so generously provided and writes a singular letter to Emory—a battering ram of a missive, dragged along by emotion, detailing where she went and what she found, scrawled in the awful, inexact script she has learned to manage with her left hand, that she knows Emory can read but few others can.

After she sets the falcon on its path, she is once again faced with her own powerlessness. Frustration boils over at the thought of inaction. How could she simply remain in her room, obediently waiting for Lady Sookhee to recover from her bout of illness, while under her feet an existential threat to humanity lurks? Unthinkable. Yeva gears up, and even as she does, she makes battle plans. Carys and Meteor, her gryphons, cannot access the dragon's abode unless she finds the opening through which the beast enters and exits

its nest. She cannot count on that possibility; she must be prepared to face it with just Sage and herself alone. It's likely to stay airborne. She should bring a bow. Does it respond to the elements? Legends name Chuan-pu as a storm dragon—if this creature is one of its descendants, should she take the flourish and fancy of mythos into account?

By the time she is thinking this, she is already striding, heavy-booted, down the wooden corridors of the palace, halfway toward the ground-floor library. The atmosphere has changed around her: a gloom seems to have descended upon the fragrant gardens, and a sense of unease charges the cold air. Where are all the servants, usually so busy and bustling? The glimpse of a wan face she catches hurrying around a corner looks mired in fear and anxiety. The peace in the royal palace has been broken by an unknown hand. It might be her own. It might be someone else's.

The entrance to the caverns is no longer unguarded. Captain Lu himself stands glowering before the offending bookshelf, an impassable bastion of wrath. His gaze narrows upon Yeva as she approaches. "You. I asked you to watch this entrance, to guard it with your life. And what did you do? Turned and went in like a little snake. You couldn't wait, could you? The very moment I trusted you with something important..."

How he knows what Yeva's been up to, she has no idea. But his fury is implacable, and Yeva has no excuses for herself. She's breached his trust. And yet—no, he never deserved it in the first place. "I found traces of a dragon living in those caverns." She flashes an iridescent scale at him, her proof of his duplicity. "As a knight of Mithrandon, I must—"

"As a knight of Mithrandon, you will do nothing. Your Emperor has no jurisdiction here. By order of our king, these caverns are not to be entered. Unless..." This time his fists tighten, as if ready to draw a weapon. "Do you wish to contest her sovereignty?"

This is not a fight Yeva knows how to have. She turns around, leaving Captain Lu to stew in his anger. But she does not return to her room. Instead, she goes up. She climbs all the way to the apex of the palace, following pathways she has come to know as well as her heart. If it is the girl-king's will that determines who goes where, then it is the girl-king's will that she must bend to her use, and damn the consequences.

Sujin snaps when she sees Yeva again. "I thought I told you—"

"I'm not waiting another day." Brusquely she shoves past the woman.

Sujin grabs her by the shoulders and blocks her with her body. But the woman is only a king's handmaiden, while Yeva is a trained knight. Yeva pushes her off easily, and when Sujin lurches to grab hold of her again, Sage comes between them, teeth bared and wings snapped out, a threat rasping in her throat. Sujin backs away from the wyrmhound with real fear in her eyes, distancing herself from Yeva until the dog's snarling ebbs into a low growl. She glances at Yeva, and Yeva has never seen such honesty in the woman's expression before this. "Don't do this. If you care for her at all . . . if she even means anything to you . . . leave it alone. Go back to your room. Forget this."

"You know I can't." With that, Yeva pushes the embroidered screens aside and strides toward the girl-king's chambers.

One fateful step, then the next. Yeva is at the threshold of Lady Sookhee's private chambers, then she crosses over.

Someone must have warned the girl-king that Yeva was coming, because Lady Sookhee waits in the middle of the room, swaying like a willow in a storm. "Yeva," she says, when she catches sight of her, and that is as far as she gets before she collapses.

Yeva lunges forward and catches her a foot off the floor. Whatever rage that filled her dissolves in a sweeping flood of alarm as Lady Sookhee slumps into her grasp. The girl-king is so bloodless, and smells so strongly of death and copper, that Yeva momentarily fears she's been assassinated, struck by a dagger to the back as she stood. But she notices the sheen of sweat on her brow and the labored breathing as though her lungs have folded in on themselves. She is ill, of course she is ill. What was Yeva thinking, barging in here when she is so unwell, rousing her and causing her upset when she is so fragile. An awful sensation sweeps Yeva, so strikingly similar to the sensation she gets when her sacred fire activates that it leaves her dizzy. In her moment of terror she wonders if this is what it means to be in love.

Guilt-stricken, Yeva carries Lady Sookhee unconscious to her bed and lays her in it. She removes her helm, her gauntlets, and places her left palm against Sookhee's forehead. The skin is cold, but she can sense the fever raging beneath it. Her mother was a healer, and as a child Yeva had begun to learn some of her craft before she left home. What she wouldn't give, in that moment, to remember any of it. To help.

Yet Lady Sookhee stirs under her touch, returning slightly to her senses. "Medicine," she whispers, through cracked lips. With a weak finger she directs Yeva to the bedside cabinet filled with little jars and unguents.

Yeva retrieves a tiny, fragile bottle filled with white powder and mixes it in a small bowl of water under her direction. "Should I call for someone—?" she asks, but Lady Sookhee demurs. She lets Yeva prepare the medicine and bring it to her, bring it to her lips. She swallows and leans back against the pillows; by the time Yeva has put away the glassware a touch of color is already returning to her face.

The sliding door flings violently aside, and standing in

its frame are Sujin, red-faced, accompanied by a furious Captain Lu. "Your Highness!"

Lady Sookhee raises a hand in gesture: everything is all right.

Sujin's eyes are cold, fixed upon Yeva like fishhooks. "Shall I have her arrested?"

"No." The girl-king forces her voice out of a hazy whisper, trembling with the effort. "Let her tend to me. We can speak later."

Sujin and Captain Lu's faces are twin studies in disbelief. "Your Highness—" Captain Lu begins.

"I understand your worries. But—" She stops to cough, spasms wracking her body. Sujin steps forward as Yeva tightens her grip on Lady Sookhee's shoulder, trying to soothe her. The girl-king shrugs them all off. "It's all right. I would like her to tend to me."

Sujin's expression tautens. She flicks a sideways glance at Yeva, heavy with distrust. They've been speaking in their native language, but now Yeva understands it, too, and Sujin can no longer conceal the meaning of her words. That knowledge shadows her face with resentment.

"Sujin," Lady Sookhee says, wearily, "I do not wish to argue about this."

Sujin and Captain Lu exchange a glance. To resist would be to go against their monarch's wishes, to lodge further complaint would only exhaust her with more quibbling. Yeva watches this understanding crystallize between them, before they bow in obeisance and, reluctantly, withdraw.

Now Yeva and the girl-king are once again alone. The uneasy sensation that bubbled in Yeva's blood is already beginning to fade, replaced with ever more guilt. She settles next to Lady Sookhee's bedside.

"You startled me, barging in like that." Lady Sookhee turns her face halfway toward Yeva's and gives her a weak smile. In that gesture is comfort and forgiveness in equal measure. "What did you want so urgently?"

"It's nothing." All of Yeva's concerns seem small and unsightly in the face of Lady Sookhee's illness. Sujin was right—the city is not burning, what could possibly be so important? What she found might not be what she thought she found. She could be mistaken. There could be some other explanation. But it can wait. It can wait two days. She runs a bare thumb over the gentle arch of Sookhee's brow. "Don't trouble yourself. We can speak when you're better."

CHAPTER NINE

OVER THE NEXT two days, Yeva tends to Lady Sookhee, intensely so, focusing every fiber of being on her care. She soaks linens in warm water and wipes the sweat from Sookhee's face. She brews healing teas and broths, drawing on wells of old knowledge long disused but not entirely dry. She eats little and sleeps at the foot of her bed. She spends the blank hours watching her lover breathe, keeping her mind free of thought by counting each inhale and exhale, measuring the distance between them, scrying meaning from every minor toss and turn. That tempest of emotion that tore through her dissipated and did not return. In its absence, in the harsh light of practicality that beats upon her like the desert sun, she finds herself doubting what she had seen in the caverns. Finds herself doubting her conclusion. Sujin comes and goes, tidying after them both, taking away spent bowls of water and fetching fresh ones. All this she does without speaking a word or meeting Yeva's eye. The other members of Sookhee's inner circle hover in the periphery, whispering amongst themselves, being quiet until out of earshot, knowing that Yeva understands their language now. The awkwardness collects around Yeva and thickens so much it feels like a clot lodged in her chest. It brings upon her a deep and sour feeling that collects in the bones of her neck, the line of her jaw. She's done this, she knows. She shouldn't have broken in. She should have known her place.

It's too many hours to herself. It lets her mind wander places it shouldn't. In the cold, cricket-filled deeps of the night, she conjures a vision of her mother, who has been absent from her mind for years as if Yeva couldn't bear to think of her. Tall and brown, with wide cheekbones and black, slicked-back hair. The haze of decades clears away, revealing sharp fragments of her childhood like glittering stones. Mother is teaching her to braid Beyar's hair, each of them taking half. Her sister hums, lost in her own worlds, happy. This was, she recalls, perhaps a year before Yeva was taken to Mithrandon. Her mother is saying, "Beloved, you will be grown soon, and you'll have to decide what kind of person you want to be." Or something along those lines. "Beloved, you don't have to answer right now, but you must think about your answer."

In this recollection Yeva doesn't hesitate. She blurts out, tugging on her sister's hair: "Of course I want to be like you, Mama!" And her mother laughs, but looks sad somehow.

More memories: her parents arguing in whispers when

the girls have been put to bed. But Yeva only pretends to sleep, eavesdropping, anxious. Even before she was sent away against her mother's will, the fissures of her parents' eventual split were already present. Her mother disapproves of Yeva learning the Empire's swordplay. "But the girl loves it so," her father says. Her mother's retort emerges as a sarcastic question: "I thought you'd left all that behind?"

But her father is right—Yeva loves the time spent in the yellow fields with the practice sword he's made for her, dodging Paul's strikes and parrying his blows, gleaming with exertion and pride as her father exclaims at how fast she learns. "You have a natural gift!" he says, a smile extending across the wide planes of his face. Yeva imagines herself heroic, defending her home and little sister from unknown threats, invaders creeping up from the tall grass and slithering through their doorways. The thought brings her joy like no other.

She thinks: Did I summon the blue fire in my blood? Did my desire bring that dragon into our house when I was a child? Could it be a choice that I made, without even realizing—a secret choice in my heart? Yeva always felt she'd had no control over the course of her life, dragged by the tides of destiny into the Empire and bound to duty before she could catch a breath. But what if she did? What if she'd turned her back on her mother and her mother's people to follow her father's path?

She aches. She can't think of her father that way, as a corrupting influence that led her away from her true self. It wasn't like that and he wasn't like that. He wasn't wrong for sending her to Mithrandon. He was doing only what he knew, what he thought best. The tragedy that is Yeva's life was sown long before that happened. It started the day when her father, lost and wounded, wandered into a village where he knew no one and barely spoke the language, and was taken in by a daughter of the village elder. Two disparate, opposing threads of destiny twined into one.

Sookhee's fever breaks on the third evening. By the fourth day she is awake, well enough to sit up. Yeva attends to her in near silence, too ashamed to speak of what happened. The girl-king whispers her thanks, wraps her hands around Yeva's when offered a cup of white peony tea. Yeva brings her bowls of congee, warm and gently seasoned with scallion oil.

"Have you eaten?" Lady Sookhee asks. "You look as awful as I feel."

Yeva does eat a little, despite the resistance from her appetite.

"What happened?" the girl-king asks. "Why did you want to see me so urgently?"

Yeva bites down on her words, unsure of how to broach the topic. She has never been a diplomat; it was Emory who was the cleverer between them, the one who knew all the right words to say at the right time. "You can't just speak your mind," he used to tell her. And right now her mind harbors more doubts than certainties; every answer seems like it could be the wrong one.

She dips into the sleeve of the generously given robes she's put back on. Her fingers close around the cool, sharp edges of the object she's looking for, which she brings into the light. A single scale which has since hardened into its final form, stiff as iron and shimmering with the same colors as the royal seal.

"I found this," she says, "in the depths of the caverns underneath the palace."

A shadow skims across the girl-king's face; quietly she puts her teacup down. "I see." And then: "I have something I must show you. But it's a place we must go to. Perhaps tomorrow, when I am feeling a little better."

Yeva nods. The opacity of the girl-king's expression reveals nothing, and the anxiety of imagining what she might mean consumes Yeva through the hours that follow. She tries to eat more, to rest well, but sleep eludes her. She finds herself lying awake in her own chambers, closing her maimed hand around the dragonscale she found. The skin on that hand is so heavily scarred it's nearly dead to sensation, but she keenly feels the presence of the precious artifact against her palm, as if there was more to it than a physical object. More to it than sharpness and inflexibility. An ache grows in her hand and creeps upward until her arm feels sore from wrist to elbow, throbbing with phantom pain.

She spends the night sleepless. In the gray slash of morning she rouses and goes to see Lady Sookhee, forcing herself past her exhaustion. As a matter of trust, she wears the fragile civilian robes that afford her no defense and leaves Varuhelt in her room, guarded by Sage. She puts on the sandalwood tiger mask that was gifted to her.

This morning Lady Sookhee is being attended by sulkpot Sujin and Kima with her long braid, the two handmaidens closest to the girl-king. Lady Sookhee is up and about, dressed again in her elaborate robes with her hair put up in a fine bun. She is paler than usual still, but her gait is steady and her back held straight. Relief surges through Yeva at seeing her recovered.

"You look like you haven't slept well," Sookhee observes, and Yeva gestures vaguely, neither confirming nor denying it. The girl-king takes her by the elbow, gently. "I promised to show you something, didn't I? Let's go."

They are meant to go unaccompanied. Sujin scowls as Yeva passes her by, but her attitude has clearly softened since their confrontation days earlier. Yeva understands that this tempered rage is the girl-king's doing, a plea to be nicer to their foreign guest despite her many transgressions. She's not sure if she'll ever be in the woman's good graces. She's not sure why she wants to be.

In the back of Lady Sookhee's private garden, hedge and bush wrap around stone steps that lead through the heart of the palace. Sookhee and Yeva follow its lightless spiral downward until they reach the ground floor, where the stairway opens directly into the royal treasury. The treasury is locked and closely guarded; Yeva has never been in it. Here are kept the kingdom's most precious artifacts and records of the royal family's history. Like a loyal dog she tails after Lady Sookhee, crossing room after room filled with precious minerals, framed calligraphy that spans a wall, painted vases taller than she is. Throughout this journey across the collected wonders of the kingdom, Sookhee says not a word, and Yeva follows her lead, staring wide-eyed and silent at the glut of history and artistry that passes her by.

Finally, they come to a wall that appears to be spanned by a single massive tapestry, a marvel of silk and ink which depicts Chuan-pu's legend, his sacrifice from which rose the kingdom of Quanbao. As Yeva takes in its towering magnificence, Lady Sookhee finally speaks. "What I'm about to show you is something that very few outside my family have been allowed to see." She glances over her shoulder. "I don't say this to scare you, or to put you in your place. Just so you know the gravity of what's before you."

She activates a hidden mechanism, pulling on a golden knob that appears to be a decorative element in the tapestry's frame. Gears turn and grind out of sight, and Lady

Sookhee steps backward as the entire wall of the archive begins to move, pivoting to reveal rock-hewn stairs that extend into dimness. The block of air that washes over them is cool and damp in a way deeply familiar to Yeva.

"Come," Lady Sookhee says, beginning the climb down those broad steps. Yeva follows, half-keen and half-weary. Already the secret door is closing behind them, grinding back into place on an automated timer. Up ahead, the way is blocked off by a slate-gray wall, upon which is carved an elaborate diorama, nine dragons converging upon a circle inscribed in the middle. Lady Sookhee draws a royal seal from her sleeve and presses it into the perfectly shaped indent within that circle. Blue light flashes in filamentous patterns, running up the shapes of the carved dragons, and the wall shudders as it withdraws into the roof like a mouth opening.

Behind them, the door to the treasury shuts completely, cutting off all light from the outside. Yeva has a sudden vision of an intruder stumbling into this secret passage, only to find it sealed and impassable at both ends, and dying a terrible and unseen death in a lightless trap. But the tunnel before them is lined with everstone emitting its cold blue light, and Yeva knows there is further to go.

They follow the pathway as it slopes gently downward. The air grows colder and their footsteps seem to drag out greater echoes. In this wordless silence, the minutes seem to stretch into hours, as if they are journeying to the center of the earth. Yeva has an inkling she is being led to a dragon's lair; she realizes it was a mistake not bringing a weapon.

"Here we are," Lady Sookhee says.

Ahead of them, the stone walls open into a vault so high it should brush the heavens. Sconces of everstone are studded along its length, illuminating a collection of wonders arrayed on stabs of stone that seem pulled up from the very ground itself. A collection of bones, scales, teeth and claws, parts of dragons long dead. Yeva draws a chilled breath, struck by a similarity—the guildknight's museum has a room like this, full of the spoils and trophies taken by hunting parties over the centuries. But while the museum back home bristled with a sense of curiosity and scientific inquiry, a greater gravity surrounds these relics, wrapped in red ribbon or raised on golden altars. On the plinth nearest to her a collection of iridescent scale—very much like that of the royal seal's—have been sewn together to make a pouch, and painted on those pearlescent leaves are words Yeva approximately recognizes as a prayer for the dead, an invocation of the veil between worlds. This is a mausoleum, a columbarium. Yeva treads carefully between each display, being very still with her breath, feeling like her very presence disturbs the sanctity of the place.

At the end of the room is a skull so large that its shape loses meaning as bone and becomes abstract, part of the terrain. Yeva doesn't even know what she's looking at until several moments in, when its lines pull together into form she recognizes. The dragon's skull is larger than a house, larger than a palace, and the beast it must have belonged to could have shaped the sky and the earth.

Sookhee sees her staring, frozen, awed, and says: "In the royal records that skull is said to be that of Chuan-pu, our ancestor dragon."

"The myth? It really happened?"

"Who's to say? In all honesty, we weren't there and we didn't see it happen, so we can never be fully certain. All we have are the records and the stories, and stories don't always have to be true. I heard a lot of stories about you before you came here. That you were cruel and deadly, an inflexible fist that crushed everything that stood in your path. But that isn't true, is it?"

The girl-king strides between the rows of dragon reliquaries. "What I can say is true, is this: dragons have always been at the center of our society and culture since time immemorial. And yes, they used to roost here in the mountains, in great numbers. Numbers that would frighten your Sun Emperor, cause him to send armies over the border. But not anymore." She looks sad. "Over the years they've been hunted as they ventured beyond our kingdom until nearly none are left. The scales you found belonged to a creature who is probably the last of her kind."

Yeva deliberately paces her words. "You've seen this creature?"

"I've not met it in these caverns myself. But I know it exists."

Yeva turns away from Sookhee. The wheels of her mind spin wildly, while her body feels cold, too heavy to move. The rage and determination she felt when she first found traces of the dragon have long fled her. It is her instinct—it is her *duty*—to hunt this creature down. But the thought of the dragon haunts her mind: this one beast, last of her kind, sliding alone through an endless dark. No one speaks to her. No one sees her. When she dies, the last of her family will go with her.

"It's a secret," she says, mostly to herself. A secret of the neighboring kingdom, well contained and well concealed. Why should it be the business of the Sun Emperor? Why should it be within Yeva's purview to get rid of it? What gives her the right?

Separate from Yeva, Lady Sookhee seems caught in her own reverie. She brushes fingers along the line of a small jawbone, almost ruefully. "It's weighed heavy on my mind for a long while now," she says. "It is during my time that this kingdom will see the end of the dragons. It's been hard to accept. Ever since the death of my royal father I haven't stopped thinking about it. In many ways it was a relief... and yet I never expected to lose my mother so soon, when I was but a young woman. Now the fate of the kingdom rests in my hands."

Something she said catches Yeva's attention. "Your royal father?" Lady Sookhee has rarely spoken of her father, much less that he was of royal status. No one in the palace has mentioned existence of a past prince-consort.

"Yes. He died a long time ago, when I was a child. It's no matter." She brushes past the topic as though ashamed of it. "When I was a young girl, I determined that I should be the last of my bloodline. I won't saddle more children with the burden of my family's curse."

"Your blood-sickness."

"Indeed. Already I planned to have a council of wise maidens rule in my stead, but I thought I had years left—I imagined I would be in my fifties when the throne fell to me. Alas, such things can never be predicted...." Briefly her gaze grows distant before she snaps back to the present. "I'm sorry for lying to you. I didn't trust you then, when you were still a stranger to our city. But I know better now. Forgive me."

You still shouldn't trust me, Yeva thinks. Guilt crashes through her, not as an avalanche but a slow glacial advance, making her bones heavy. If she had to choose between her duty and the tender shoots of affection that have grown in her over the past few months, which would she pick? She has no answer to that. "It is me who needs to ask forgiveness," she says. "I behaved rudely, especially to Sujin. And Captain Lu."

"Understanding will come in time," she says. "But now you know this secret which we have been keeping from you. Far be it from me to tell you what to do, but I do dearly hope that you will keep this secret a little while longer."

Yeva thinks of the falcon she sent to Emory, and the guilt advances deeper into her bones. "Of course," she says. She will write to Emory again, in cold and clear terms, telling him it was all a misunderstanding, telling him she now understands the situation through a lens of logic and there is nothing to worry about. He will read her letter and concede to her deductions, canceling whatever preparations he has been making since her prior, barely coherent missive. It will all blow over. It has to.

CHAPTER TEN

OVER THE NEXT weeks, Yeva settles into an unease that masquerades as stillness, that uninformed observers might even think is peace. The moment her falcon returns, she writes that promised, sober letter to Emory telling him to disregard everything she previously said—"all will be explained when I return to Mithrandon," she says in parting. She thinks, *if I return to Mithrandon,* but that thought no longer fills her with excitement as it once did. She has, in the past months, started to imagine a different future for herself, one where she left the guild and came to live in Daqiao permanently. One where she remained lover and confidante to the girl-king for the rest of her days. But these thoughts now seem inappropriate. Yeva returns to her place by Lady Sookhee's side, an awkward addition to the court, a cherished intimate to the girl-king yet a stranger from a hostile empire. But their relationship is irrevocably changed. The connection between them has been tainted by complex matters, contaminated by thoughts of duty and kinghood and Imperial greed spreading like mold. Within Yeva a pendulum swings between complex emotions she can't quite name—some days she thinks she feels despair, and other days it's rage, but one thing she knows is that she isn't happy. She misses, with an unwarranted ferocity, the earlier days of her time in Daqiao, when she had grown drunk on new language and custom, intoxicated by freedom, nostalgia, the apricot flush of intimacy. She hopes her letter to Emory will be enough. She hopes the damage can be undone.

For her part, Lady Sookhee behaves as if Yeva's transgressions had never happened, as if she had never broken into sacred spaces or threatened those closest to her, as if she herself hadn't hid the truth of the beast living in the mountains from Yeva. She acts as if the knot of deception and mistrust between them can be sunk to the bottom of a river and forgotten. For which Yeva is grateful. She, too, pretends nothing has happened. She greets Captain Lu in the mornings as she always has. She takes lunches with his lieutenants, even if the easy flow of conversation notably dips when she is around. She remains genial with Sookhee's handpicked council. One evening, in response to something Yeva said about flowers for an upcoming prayer day, Sujin snorts and says, "Trust you, Soup Ladle, to always pick the most roundabout method." She speaks with utmost derision, but the nickname comforts Yeva anyway. She still remembers. She still hasn't given up on Yeva's place in the palace.

Still, the unease remains. After speaking so openly about the kingdom's secrets in the dragon mausoleum, Lady Sookhee closes up like an iron door which Yeva can't prize back open. Her stack of questions have only multiplied since that morning, and there are no answers to be found. She fears that asking them will shatter the precarious peace she's been allowed. She tries her own investigation, but her sources are few: she can't very well go poking around the already wary royal household. She tries the libraries, but her comprehension of the written language is still too poor to make much of it. It was easier for her to pick up speaking and listening, to deal with immediacies and intimacies, than it is with the dry academia of court records and official histories.

At Aunty Anuya's that week, she asks: "What do you know of Lady Sookhee's royal father? She's mentioned him in passing to me, but I can't find anything written about him."

"A royal father?" Aunty Anuya looks confused. "I'm not sure about that. The late king never married, and she never had any lovers—not that I knew of, anyway. She didn't seem like the kind who was like that. There's a rumor that she conceived her daughter with a passing merchant, some traveler from another country. But, aiya—" She gets up to fetch a fresh pot of water, which she thumps down upon on the table. "Such things you should be asking your lady, not me."

"I see." But of course Yeva can't ask Lady Sookhee these

questions. She'll get a non-answer, or silence, or a lie. All three would be worse than not knowing. So she remains suspended in ignorance. In this uncertainty her mind starts stitching together story after speculative story. She imagines Lady Sookhee's royal father—a pale and narrow man in her imagination, no thicker than a pane of glass—running from the royal palace to become a recluse in the misty mountains, digging himself into the damp earth, never to be seen again. She invents origins for each of the tasseled lanterns hung over Sookhee's bed, imagining them gifts from loyal subjects or foreign dignitaries. And while in bed she stares at the long pink scar running down the left side of Sookhee's ribs, which she fashions into a long-forgotten assassination attempt. A knife in the dark, plunging into the side of a child's body, stopped at the last crucial moment by the guards outside. Yeva runs her fingers down the whorled knots of flesh, and Sookhee deliberately pushes her hand away, frowning. Neither speak, but Yeva senses the emotional fragility of the moment and withdraws her hand. Lady Sookhee looks away, but something in her blink reminds Yeva of a snake, membrane sliding over a glassy eye.

Day after day, she goes about feeling like a soap bubble carried upon the wind, liable to burst at the lightest touch. In the center of her being lies an absence where home and family should be. Her years in Mithrandon had hollowed her out, and she had filled that void with duty and obedience; now that those things have been stripped from her like limestone leached out of bedrock, she fears she might crumble under the weight of nothingness.

When she sleeps, Yeva has dreams of every dragon she's ever slain. Over the years, she has killed a hundred of their kind in every shape and size, from lowly worms the length of her foot to elders big as a mountain. Each one she remembers with great exactness: every fight is a life extinguished at the edge of her blue blade, something taken out of the universe. She makes endings and she mustn't forget. As she lies with her eyes closed, they appear in a rippling swarm, a hundred flashes of scale and sinew, a thousand shining teeth and tongues. Their breath is hot upon her skin. The yearling with silver horns, whom she slew upon becoming a guildknight, dances once again, its fire blossoming against obsidian night. The ice queen, who trapped her on a snowy mountain and very nearly escaped its fate, slides glacial fingers along the knots of her spine. Her first stumbling and uncertain kill, the lithe wyrm from her childhood, curls around her ankle. Floating weightless through a black void, Yeva welcomes them all into her arms, into her body. They form a vortex, pressing their thick, sinuous bellies against hers until she can no longer pick out the border where she ends and the dragons begin. She moves and they, too, move in concert. As the dream proceeds, Yeva becomes certain that their limbs are her limbs, their clever jaws her clever jaws. She runs across the curve of the planet on clawed feet, a flame beneath her ribs and golden blood in her chest. She becomes so enormous she blots out the sun. She finds herself on the banks of the Yalo, being pursued by a party of guildknights from the Sun Empire. She drowns them all in the frigid curtains of the river, all save one. On those mornings, Yeva wakes coated with sweat and trembling like a leaf, fighting to separate the dream from reality.

The awkwardness between her and the girl-king grows. Yeva accumulates anxieties and wild theories like rocks in her head, while Lady Sookhee seems more and more preoccupied by unspoken problems, drawing deeper into herself, shrouded with worries. Every now and then she catches the girl-king staring at her like Yeva is a puzzle that needs to be solved, but these glances are fleeting, and the girl-king looks away the moment she notices Yeva staring back, as if ashamed. The situation is becoming unbearable.

Almost a month after Lady Sookhee's revelation, she calls Yeva to her chambers at night. Yeva finds her standing in the garden, back turned to her, hands clasped to her chest. She is paler than usual and her breaths are quick and fevered. "Your illness," Yeva says, in alarm. It's about that time. "You should be resting, or it'll get worse."

The girl-king cannot meet her eyes. "I have something to tell you," she begins.

"It can wait until after your illness passes."

"No. No, it can't wait." Lady Sookhee pulls herself up and finally looks directly at Yeva. "It has to do with my illness, Yeva. And it has to do with the questions I am sure you have begun to ask yourself. There are things I have been keeping from you that I no longer want to hold secret. Yeva, there are things that you need to know about me."

Around Yeva the world has started to warp, the air closing in, the ground tilting. "What things?"

Sookhee draws a deep breath, her body visibly shaking—whether from impending illness or from fear, Yeva cannot tell. She waits for the girl-king to speak, for her lover to spill forth her burden that will fix every doubt Yeva has, that will knit every wound back into flesh. She opens her mouth. She begins: "The truth is, I—"

"Lady!" It's Kima, rushing in, her face white except for two spots of exertion on her cheeks. It's clear she has run a long way: her chest heaves with frantic breath. "Knights, at the city gates!"

"Have they reached us already?" Lady Sookhee presses a hand to her throat, and Yeva thinks she looks like she might faint. "It's sooner than I expected. . . ."

Yeva takes her by the elbow. "What do you mean?" Knights—guildknights—this must be her doing. The Emperor has decided to send a garrison after all. "Did you know they were coming?"

"They crossed the border earlier today," Lady Sookhee

says. Tremors continue to run through her slender frame. "I thought we would have more time...."

"Guildknights travel fast," Yeva says. "Our gryphons are quicker than ordinary horses."

"What shall we do?" Kima asks.

"We must welcome them." Even through her weakness Lady Sookhee remains ever the monarch, resolute and determined. "Kima, make preparations. I will give them an audience before I go into seclusion. Hurry."

"Yes," Kima says, and she goes, almost running, robes hitched up.

Yeva asks: "Is this what you were going to tell me?"

"No." Lady Sookhee sags sideways in exhaustion. Her hands go to her hips, as if it's the only thing keeping her upright. "It was something else. Now's not the time. Yeva, we might not get to speak again before I go into seclusion. I have only one thing to beg of you: do not let those soldiers into the cavern. I know that's what they're here for. Find some way to stall them. Until—"

"Until the danger has passed?"

She nods. "Until then. Now go—surely you'll want to meet them at the gate."

Yeva does, but she can't meet them like this. They would not recognize her. She cannot reveal this much of herself to them. Her first stop is to her room, to change into her knight's garb: the mail, the helm, the heraldry. Piece by piece it goes on, aided by her much-neglected contraptions. She fumbles. A gauntlet slips as she struggles to put it on. She's out of practice; her hands have already started to forget the motions she performed daily for a good part of her life. The weight upon her feels unnatural now, clogging her movements with their bulk. She can't imagine how she spent so much of her life with this burden upon her shoulders. Her hands shake as she puts the helmet back over her head. Yeva has forgotten how dark it was within its metal confines, how echoey and distorted. She feels a stranger in her own body.

Yeva meets the Empire's party as they come up the Main Street to the royal palace. His Radiance has not sent a full garrison, thank the goddess, but a hunting party of four guildknights, each with their attendants, and a wagon for provisions following in the back. Together they form a clot of noise moving up the cobbled street as people hover warily in the shelter of storefronts, watching this parade with an air of suspicion. How out of place the Empire's guildknights look, bright and uncouth, armor clanking and clashing, obnoxious banners held aloft.

At the head of the group, perched on a dappled mare with dove-gray wings, is Emory. Not wrapped in the soft linings of velvet and silk she's used to, but in shining breastplate with his family's heraldry laid over it. She's never seen him look so martial, so formidable. "Emory," she says, running beside her cousin's mount, reaching up to tug on the reins, feeling like nothing more than a small child. "Emory!"

He glances downward with his expression pinched and severe. "Yeva."

"Why are you here? Why did you come?"

"Why else?" Now he looks annoyed. "You wrote that the King of Quentona is harboring a dragon, Yeva. I'm here because of you."

※

THE NEXT HOURS tumble onward, in their horrible way. The guildknights are taken to their lodgings, while Emory, as their leader, is led to the Great Phoenix Hall for an audience with the girl-king. Yeva accompanies her guildmaster, a silent observer tailing in his shadow as he bends the knee, just as she did so many months ago. Unlike Yeva, he has come with a speech prepared, florid and flattering, seeking the grace of Her Majesty to—

Lady Sookhee raises her hand. "Enough," she says, through wheezing lungs. "We know why your guildknights have come, we know what they seek. These are matters that should be discussed later. As you can see, I am not well. Your knight—Yeva—can explain these matters to you. I greet you, as a courtesy, but any further talk must wait. We shall speak again in a few days, when I have recovered."

Emory looks up. "I understand the nature of Your Majesty's health, but—"

"That is all that needs to be said. You may go."

With that summary dismissal, Lady Sookhee stands without waiting for Emory's reply. She sways as she does so, the grasping fingers of her illness draining the strength from her body. Kima leaps forward to catch her, to support her as she totters toward the exit. Sujin, who has glowered watchfully from the sidelines, comes forward to wedge her body between Emory and the royal dais, blocking the view of her king's weakness from these foreigners.

Emory is too much of a diplomat to openly contest the will of the girl-king. But Yeva sees sullenness in him as he stands. He gestures. "Come."

At this moment she feels like she might split in two. Half her instincts scream out their desire to run after Lady Sookhee, to make sure she's all right, to help Kima settle her in her sickbed. The other half, the more sensible half, wants to cleave to the habits she's cultivated all her life. Her captain calls for her. She is a soldier of the Sun Empire, she must follow.

Within her helm, Yeva shuts her eyes. The old weight of her armor, the syllables of the language that Emory barks at her: it's all coming back, wrapping her in a cold shroud of reality. It drags her downward into an older version of Kunlin Yeva, one who is the famed masked guildknight of Mithrandon, who knows duty and knows duty only. Has she forgotten? She's acting as though she has never been allowed to tend to Lady Sookhee when her blood-sickness is in full swing. If she had gone after Kima, Sujin would have stopped her anyway. *Know your place.*

Emory has been given a room neighboring Yeva's, directly across the courtyard they both share. Within it, his boy Telken is running to-and-fro, unpacking, getting his master's affairs in order. "Telken," he says heavily, "let us have some privacy."

The boy scuttles out of the room, dipping his head to Yeva in greeting as he goes. Leaving Yeva and Emory alone in a room for the first time since she left Mithrandon, which seems a different lifetime, lived by somebody else. Yeva hesitates before pulling her helm off her head, inhaling air spiced with ripening summer fruit.

Emory looks exhausted, as if he has walked all the way from Mithrandon on foot. "What mess have you gotten us into, Yeva?"

"It isn't my mess," she says. "I told you not to come. There's nothing to see; I told you I was mistaken. Why did you come anyway?"

"Why did I—" Emory stamps a small, petulant circle, pulling his fingers through his hair. "Goddess above, Yeva. You wrote a panicked missive declaring you'd found a dragon living in the massive caverns underneath the city, then followed it with a ridiculous letter saying never mind, I was wrong, don't come here, it was nothing. What was I to think?" He grows still, serious. His voice drops. "You're not under duress, are you? Please, Yeva. You can tell me."

"I am not." Her heart is tumbling sideways; she never considered that Emory would draw that conclusion. Certainly her letters have glossed over the private aspects of her relationship with the girl-king, but she'd only ever written good things about her time here. "I must have represented Quanbao poorly in my writings for you to think so little of Lady Sookhee. She has been nothing but kind to me."

"I see."

"You shouldn't be here, Emory. Everything's fine. Go home."

"Go home?" Emory looks like he's swallowed a lemon slice, and he turns away. He picks up an oddly shaped trunk, an oblong thing the right size and shape to hold a rolled-up rug. But it contains no carpeting: as he places it on the low desk that obstructs the middle of the room, it thumps as if filled with metal. "Go home, you say. Yeva, His Radiance has gotten involved. He wants results, he wants trophies."

"Trophies." Her mouth is dry, her lips feel like cracking. "A man who hunts on His Radiance's lands is liable to lose his head. Why does he think he can do the same under some other monarch's rule?"

Emory's fingers grip the edges of the table hard. "You

speak as if we hunt some fleet four-footed creature, not a monster that could destroy a village with a single breath."

"The dragons in Quanbao are spiritual beasts. They don't hunt. They don't destroy villages."

"Is that what they've told you?" Emory flips the lid of his trunk. "Is that what you believe?"

Within an interior of red velvet padding is the device he was working on when she saw him last. He hefts it in his arms, and for the first time Yeva recognizes it for what it is: a weapon. A musket of some sort. He points the muzzle away from her, and she catches a glimpse of his completed handiwork along the length of the tube. A fist of everstone sits within the musket's core, and thin lines of blue run along the weapon's machinery. Emory thumbs a switch and the weapon hums, coming alive the way Varuhelt does. Even though Emory doesn't have the holy gift that Yeva does. Even though he shouldn't be able to activate it.

Yeva's blood thrums in her neck, twinging along her shoulders. He's created a sacred weapon that anyone can use. She's not sure how he's done it, but she thinks of all the time he's spent holed up in his tower in experimentation and research, sometimes to the detriment of his duty as guildmaster. And the Emperor's largesse toward this dereliction. Now she understands why. With this musket, any ordinary soldier in the Imperial army will be able to wield the power of the everstone.

She thinks: I told them of the garden of everstone I found under the city. I've whetted His Radiance's appetite for conquest.

Emory says: "You saw the report on the attack years ago, didn't you? I read my father's notes on this and discovered details that were not reflected in the official record. There were two dragons sighted that day. A younger one, not yet full-grown, which was wounded, and an adult that swept in to protect it. Both fled toward the border after killing a half dozen of our men." His face tightens, as if to say *this would not have happened on my watch. I would have made sure that things were recorded properly.* She cannot recognize this version of her cousin who stands before her. Emory's face is unreadable as he says, "The girl-king has not been forthright with you, Yeva. Those caves must harbor a population of dragons that she's concealing. Breeding pairs and family groups. We have to take a look, at least."

Yeva says, "The girl-king has forbidden entrance to the caverns while she is in seclusion. To defy her orders is to contest her will. Is His Radiance prepared to go to that extent?"

"You already know the answer to that."

"And are you?"

Emory doesn't reply. He runs his fingers along the surface of his musket as though stroking the head of a dog. "The entrance to the caverns. You know where it is, don't you?"

"We can't go in. It's impossible. I've lost the key."

He glances sideways at her and sighs. "Yeva. You're a terrible liar."

"Don't make me do this," she pleads. She knows that if he insists, if he says *that's an order,* she'll do what he says. Because that's what she's been trained to do. And Emory knows this too. It's a weapon in his arsenal that he's never used. He knows that doing so will reshape their relationship forever.

Her cousin sighs. Her captain closes the lid of his trunk and calls loudly for Telken. The servant boy stumbles in through the screen door as Yeva hastily pushes her helm back on her head.

"Summon the others," Emory tells him. "We must make plans."

CHAPTER ELEVEN

THE MEN EMORY has chosen for this mission are not Mithrandon's best. There's Joufren of Windbyrn, an old knight whose long career in the guild was remarkably undistinguished, and who one assumes was given a captaincy in his old age out of pity. Answering to him are Ferrel and Dewitt, two hotheads, almost like brothers in their temperament, more arrogance than ability. The last member of their party is Keltan, a sallow youth, a farmer's boy who was thought to have the gift of the blood, but was never able to wield the holy weapons. To make up for that lack, he turned sharp-eyed for weaknesses and sharp-tongued to pick people apart at the seams. They regard the masked guild-knight with a wariness that borders on resentment, preemptively accusing her of stealing their moment of glory. As they barrel into Emory's room one after another, the air thickens with their oaths and chatter, and for the first time in months Yeva is surrounded by thoughts unapologetically expressed in Thrandish. Instead of filling her with nostalgia, it clogs her with dread. She is once again a child, alone in a room full of trainees whispering about her. She thought that old lesion of inadequacy had long scabbed over, but her months in Daqiao have softened and dissolved those scars, once again exposing her tender flesh. The guildknights are rude and dismissive of everything they've seen in the country, calling it primitive, a shithole, and other less polite things.

"Let's just slay this beast and go," Ferrel says. "I'll do someone an injury if I am forced to linger here and eat the dung they call food."

Keltan curls his lip and sneers, "That silken whore on the throne is ill, isn't she? Now's our chance," and it's all Yeva can do to keep herself from flying across the room and choking him until his speckled face turns puce.

"Enough," Emory snaps. "Like it or not, the girl-king is sovereign ruler here and must be treated with the esteem afforded to all of her station. To disrespect one monarch is to disrespect them all. Do you understand?"

The men shrink like scolded schoolboys; even their captain seems cowed by Emory's anger. For a cousin of the Sun Emperor, he is a meek man, who simply nods in agreement as Emory lays out his plans for the hunt, drawing up a formation. Keltan ahead, with Ferrel and Dewitt in the middle, and Joufren and Emory bringing up the rear. Leading them all will be Yeva, who knows the way.

"Once we reach the caverns," Emory says, "the wyrmhounds will track our quarry down."

"Oh, but Sage is unwell right now," Yeva says, thinking fast. "She can't hunt, we will have to wait."

Keltan responds, smirking: "That's all right. We've brought our own."

As Emory lays out attack sequences for when they find their target, based on what he has learned about southern dragons, Yeva realizes that he had been quietly preparing this for months. The sense of betrayal bruises her in the ribs. She had thought they were in agreement, that they were both dedicated to the subtle task of directing the Sun Emperor's covetous fingers away from Quanbao. Barring her one misstep, Yeva thought she had kept faithfully to this goal. Meanwhile Emory, it seems, had been preparing for war.

He turns to her. "Yeva, what do you think?"

She blinks and swallows. In the hurt and uncertainty of this revelation, all of her convictions dissolve into old brine. Old habit and comfortable structure rush to take their place. She is a blade of Empire, an obedient weapon that acts as she is directed. "I will do as you wish."

✵

SO TO THE ground floor the party goes, Yeva guiding them through the corridors, ushering them so they avoid the eyes of servants on the way, until they come to the library, the shelf, the hidden stairs that lead to the unseen depths. At the door stands Captain Lu with his spear, angry and watchful, and Yeva's heart grows heavy. Emory had said, "Let me take charge of this part," but she knows he will never convince Captain Lu to go quietly. Perhaps this is a good thing, their plans foiled before they can begin. But Captain Lu will see her, has seen her, and already his expression makes it clear how much further she has fallen in his estimation. His eyes narrow. "What is the meaning of this?"

Emory steps forward. He's strapped the musket across his chest, and now he holds it in his arms, muzzle pointing forward, a clear threat. "We came to your country to investigate these tunnels. Let us through."

Captain Lu's grip on his spear tightens. "You dare?"

"Let us through," Emory repeats.

Yeva's stomach tightens and sinks to the bottom of the ocean. Captain Lu is facing a hunting party of guildknights, fully armed, and their wyrmhounds. She watches that knowledge register in his eyes. But still they are in the palace itself, in the heart of the city, utterly outnumbered. Captain Lu draws a deep breath to summon reinforcements.

Quick as a snake Emory lunges forward and thrusts the muzzle of his weapon into Captain Lu. Blue light strobes like lightning and Captain Lu folds, a cotton sheet crumpling to the ground. Yeva shouts. "What have you done?"

Emory's face is very white, but the line of his jaw is set. "He's not dead. He's knocked out, he'll wake with a headache, but nothing worse. Don't worry, I've tested it."

She stares at Captain Lu's inert form, his jaw slack, his spear useless beside him, and grows dizzy. "Tested it? What on?"

Emory looks away. "Just open the door. Hurry, before someone comes."

"What have you made?"

"Yeva." He slings the musket over his shoulder. "Open the door."

She should resist. If she had a mind of her own she would run, call for more guards, use her knowledge of the palace layout to escape Emory's party and find help. But that's not who she is. Within her armor her body burns with anger and uncertainty, but still she follows the orders given by her captain, tame as ever, well-trained if not well-bred. Pride of the Empire. The secret door opens, the secret pathway is revealed. The caverns deep beneath the earth await them.

"It's dark down there," Dewitt says. He sounds uncertain.

Emory is unimpressed. "Don't lose your nerve. Ferrel, light a torch. Keep moving forward, soldier."

Down, down, down they go. The atmosphere chokes them like a hand that rises from the grave. The guildknights' wyrmhounds run ahead, their small talons clicking rapidly against stone as they gambol, sniffing the air. Yeva's insides churn. She doesn't need the wyrmhounds' excitement to tell her that their prey is close: the blood sings in her veins, thrumming in concert with that of a nearby dragon's. The creature whose traces she found a month ago is somewhere in this cavern, unaware that hunters are coming to cut it down.

She feels sick. A hundred hunts she has carried out in her short life, each one of them righteous. But this feels deplorable, an expedition built upon lies and riddled with transgressions. She's seeing a side to Emory that is new to her, that she has already begun to loathe. Everything about what she is doing right now is a mistake. She takes them through the pathway she knows well, that she can navigate with her eyes closed, but she really shouldn't.

The light warms into orange as they approach the lava falls, and the cool air turns hostile, agitated. Behind her Keltan makes noises of dismay. "How are we to make it past this inferno?"

Emory hushes him. To Yeva he says: "Lead the way."

Yeva carefully treads along the lava's edge toward the hidden crack in the wall. A wild thought seizes her, that she should push the rest of the hunting party into the boiling pits of molten firmament and flee before anyone can stop her. Who would register such a crime? But she keeps moving, one foot in front of another. Maybe the portal has been bricked over in the month since she's discovered it.

But no such luck. There it is, a jagged sideways mouth in the black rock, and like a sheep Yeva leads the other knights through it, their wyrmhounds nipping at her heels as though it is she they are hunting. Behind her the knights make jibes about their situation to ease the tension, to substitute sarcasm for courage. Ferrel says, "So that was the danger that made these caverns impassable to all? A haze of fire? Pathetic, the worms living in this country are even weaker than I thought."

Keltan snorts. "You speak like you wouldn't catch fire if you fell in," and in reply Ferrel slings at him an oath that would melt the skin off a person.

Dewitt says, uncharacteristically thoughtful: "These magma falls cannot be the reason the caverns were closed off, and with such regularity too. I suspect the whore queen must be hiding the passage of a dragon that visits regularly. Her beloved pet, perchance?"

"Be quiet," says Captain Joufren.

Unease grows in Yeva. For once she agrees with the men: there was never any real danger here. The secrecy around the caves is for the sake of the dragon who lingers here, the dragon who passes through these hollows almost every month, like clockwork. That can be the only reason. The watchfulness of the palace staff, the protectiveness with which they keep people from entering the caves... an alarm builds in her mind, a scatter of thoughts coalescing into a single picture that trembles just out of focus—there is a story here, and she's on the cusp of understanding it.

The walls of rock release them into the city-sized canyon that Yeva had discovered, studded with clumps of everstone. Sharp intake of air behind her as the hunting party take in the sight. Even old Joffrey cannot help himself, exclaiming: "Such quantity of the stone as I have never seen—!"

"Hush," says Emory suddenly, and at that moment a strange wind howls through the air, as if in the distance something enormous moves through at terrible speed. Scenting prey, each wyrmhound darts forward with a single bark of warning, like arrows loosed from a bowstring.

"Look sharp," Emory says. "Our quarry approaches!"

They run, following the hounds. Far above their heads, the silver roof of the cavern yawns. Yeva doesn't need a wyrmhound to tell her where a dragon is: that knowledge keens in her blood, a sense of specific distance and speed, not seen but felt. But this time her perception of their quarry bears a particular terror that tweaks her recognition, a metallic tang that seems familiar and she doesn't know why. The dragons she hunts are strangers to her but this one is not.

Fear builds in her heart. She runs with Varuhelt gripped in her sword hand, the claw that poets call the talon of the

Empire. It is too late to turn back. Their target has realized this too: at some point in their pursuit it had stopped fleeing and turned around. The distance between them closes rapidly. Is it coming to attack them? Or cornered, has it decided to put up a fight? Yeva thinks it's neither. Resignation saddles the connection between them, hunter and her prey. The creature they chase is tired of running, tired of hiding. It is turning to meet its fate.

Keltan shouts, a noise of fear: they've spotted it. In the gloomy distance, rapidly growing huge, a tangle of white writhes and loops through the air. A southern dragon like the one depicted in the tapestry. The air turns frigid and violent; lightning crackles in the air as their lungs fill with stinging ice. A storm dragon, harbinger of tempests. Yeva has hunted creatures that were masters of elements, but nothing like this: a force of nature, brushing against godhood, shimmering in the same blues and pinks of the royal seal Yeva has come to know so well. Those branching horns glow white and yellow as though made of the lightning itself. The beast has the size and strength to topple walls and crush towers by winding around it, and yet its body could easily fit through the eye socket of the giant skull Yeva was shown.

The dragon arcs in high circles around their heads. The hunting party clumps in terror, buffeted by the sudden gales. "Do something," Keltan howls at her. "Aren't you the famous masked guildknight?"

At this point Yeva realizes none of the party have any experience hunting full-grown dragons. Emory's battle plan, conceived and explained in dry, light-filled rooms, dissolves in the face of vicious reality, rimed with ice and howling with wind so loud it blots out all thought. The men grip their weapons, frozen by terror. Only Emory has his musket raised, buzzing with harsh light, eyes flickering frantically as he watches the dragon's wild passage, unable to find a good shot.

"Do something," Keltan shouts again, but this time full-throated in his uselessness. Worse than useless. He doesn't understand. Yeva never fights dragons in the air, where they are the masters and she at a disadvantage. If they won't come down, her gryphons and wyrmhound work in concert to ground them, tearing at wing and limb until they have no choice. It's dangerous work, but quite rarely required: dragons are ferocious beasts who leap at every challenge to their territory. They come to Yeva, drawn to the sapphire scent of her blood. But this one is different. It swoops over them, freezing air as it goes, and there it stays, out of reach. Yeva hasn't brought her gryphons, or Sage. Neither has she brought her bow. She would have prepared far better for her own hunts, but this is not a hunt she wanted. But the dragon does not want to fight either. A wailing, terrible impasse has set in.

And then she sees it. Curving along the dragon's side: a

long, slashing scar. Distinct even in the unstable light of the cavern. Yeva recognizes its shape. She knows this particular knot of flesh.

The last piece of the mystery slides into place. Yeva sucks in freezing air as the ground falls away in her mind, tipping her into a polar ocean that is so clear, so bright, and from her new, upside-down refracted perspective everything suddenly makes sense, it all makes sense. The dragon—I know you, I know who you are. She bursts forward, running, her limbs having a will of her own. She must see the scar clearly. She has to make sure.

But in her heart, she already knows. The truth—the final truth, the thing that Lady Sookhee was about to confess to her the night before, the thing she was about to say before they were interrupted.

Behind her Emory screams something that the wind swallows; his muffled syllables are just sound, only sound. Yeva races ahead, away from the party, away from whatever she should care about. The striated belly of dragon soars above her head, and she wants to shout, come down here, show me who you are, show me now! Her blood calls to the dragon, or is it the other way around? Hasn't their blood pulsed in concert as they lay together at night?

Behind her noise and thunder erupt. Emory sets off his musket and the cavern fills with lightning whiter than the blue flame. Not the small jab he'd felled Captain Lu with but a burst of divine wrath. The storm dragon shrieks and tilts as a blue bolt strikes it, but in the charged air it is not just the dragon that gets hit. The blue fire arcs from rock outcrop to rock outcrop, shattering stalactite and fracturing the cavern's vault. Stone cracks and the roof of the cavern collapses with a horrible roar. The ground shakes as if splitting to swallow them whole, and Yeva stumbles, crashing into the dirt.

But death doesn't come for her in jaws of falling rock or whipping tongues of lava, and Yeva regains her feet to find only mounds of rubble behind her, no sound or sight of the hunting party. Waves of nameless emotion roil through the length of her body. She moves as though in a dream, and perhaps she is in a dream, a nightmare of her own making. She is not sure which way is up or down anymore.

Ahead of her, wounded but still alive, the shimmering dragon flees into the dark. That way lies the real answers to all the questions she has been asking. That way she must go. Yeva picks up her feet, makes her body respond to her again. She runs after the thing she has been hunting.

CHAPTER TWELVE

AT ITS FAR end, the cavern splits off into several smaller hollows through which groundwater rushes, reflecting the light of the everstone, twinkling like fireflies, like a fairy grotto. In this dreamlike diorama the storm dragon has come to rest, taking refuge in the largest of the hollows. Its ropelike body coils in loops upon the rocks, sides heaving with exertion. Yeva cautiously draws near, one slow step after another, and it allows her approach. The tempestuous air has quieted; small sparks of lightning still travel down the dragon's yellow horns, but Yeva no longer feels like she's about to be blown off a mountainside. She finally has free rein to study this otherworldly creature up close.

The dragon's body is covered in the same sort of iridescent scale that Yeva has carried about in a silken knot for several months. The first four of its six limbs are taloned like a gryphon's, but the last two are enormous paddles like a leviathan's. Diaphanous membranes flare from its spine and tail and clawed limbs, a creamy magnolia shade. And there's its great, finned head, tapering to a fine snout, crowned by its lightning horns. Along its side is the scar that Yeva knows so well. In the presiding calm, Yeva is allowed to gaze at it all she wants, and any doubt about the crazy notion she's developed is dispelled. She knows this scar. She knows who it belongs to.

The beast watches Yeva intently, its great yellow eyes never flickering. There's nothing of Lady Sookhee in its canny face, no trace of humanity in its shape or expression. Yeva wonders what it feels like. To lose yourself so completely, to become something else entirely. To be so changed. What does it think? What does she feel? It makes sense that these transformations take so much out of the girl-king, that she is sick for days before and after.

Yeva is close enough to touch the dragon. Its breath washes over her, a great warm tide that raises the hairs on the back of her neck. Yeva slowly removes her helm, places it upon the damp slate at her feet. She pulls free the gauntlet on her scarred hand, thrusting that gnarled skin into the open air. Tentatively, as though she expects to be jolted, she reaches her hand forward until carefully, gently, it brushes against the bright scales of the dragon's snout. A jolt does run up her arm then, but not one of electricity; she shudders with a sense of recognition, of relief, of elation. A potent mix of the three. The dragon makes a sound like the cry of the wind through castle walls on a winter's night.

"I know who you are," Yeva says. "You don't have to hide from me."

Their eyes meet and a shiver runs through the great beast lying before her. Understanding and trust pass between them, fragile wordless things like a leaf on a lake, like snow on a windowpane.

A seismic tremble runs through the dragon's bones and light fills the hollow. Its luminance brings neither heat nor cold but a gentle whisper like a murmuration of spring petals through the air. Even within her armor Yeva feels bathed. Before her, the wounded dragon transforms. Its scales shed from its skin, showering the ground with radiance. Its limbs shrink and its body collapses upon itself, curling into a comma, a tiny human figure. When the light fades, Lady Sookhee crouches unclothed, clutching a burned arm, gaze fixed upon the ground, trembling with exertion.

Yeva finds it in her body to move. She kneels beside her lover, stiff in the armor she cannot take off without aid. She lays her bare hand on the girl-king's forehead. Cold, as it always is when her blood-sickness takes hold. Or what she called her blood-sickness, although Yeva knows its true nature now. "You're all right," she manages, the words clumsy and surreal against their backdrop.

Sookhee's voice is hoarse, as if clawing its way out of a long, dark tunnel. "When did you realize?"

"Only just now." She hesitates, thinking. "Although I

suppose, deep down, I have always suspected something like this."

"Did you, now?"

"I'm not as shocked as I ought to be."

Water drips in the cavern. The stillness and silence stand in stark contrast to the apocalyptic furor of their confrontation when Sookhee had been a dragon. "So now you know. The true nature of my periodic illness. Why we have to seal off the caverns every month. I must transform to balance the energy of this, my other form. This is a secret that few outside the walls of the palace know. The people only know the myths and stories, they have no idea how close to the truth it is."

"Is this the secret you were trying to tell me?"

"It was." Sookhee shifts her weight, kneeling fully upon the ground. "Forgive me. I know it was wrong to withhold this information, especially after I showed you the mausoleum. But—"

"But I am a guildknight of Mithrandon, a dragon-hunter of great renown. There was no reason to think I wouldn't see you as an abomination."

"Indeed."

Yeva closes her scarred hand into a fist; she feels the blue fire in her blood, that glowing ember of supernatural power that hangs in the shadows of her life, quiet and waiting until she calls upon it, waking it into cleansing inferno.

She unhooks Varuhelt from her waist and activates its fiery blade, casting azure light into the darkest corners of the caverns.

She thinks: this strange gift of mine, which they say is holy, which they say comes from sources beyond the veil of the mortal world—if I learned to wield it correctly, might I also turn into a dragon?

She says: "No more of an abomination than I am."

Sookhee gets to her feet, stumbling in exhaustion. Yeva darts forward to catch her, hold her steady. It feels like a routine they've had forever, as though they were born to do this. "Let me show you something," she says.

She totters toward the back of the hollow; it's a long way to walk for someone so fragile. Yeva holds her steady.

The thing she wants to show Yeva is a dragon skull hoisted on an altar of stone, surrounded by teeth of everstone. A reasonably sized thing, belonging to a beast of similar size to Sookhee when she transforms. Like the relics in the royal mausoleum, ribbons have been wrapped around the altar, and knotted rope hangs between two everstone tips, from which bronze bells dangle. Other bones have been carefully placed around the altar: a handful of vertebrae and talons in radial patterns, and pairs of curving ribs form a protective frame over them.

Sookhee comes to stop before this diorama, leaning heavily on Yeva for balance. "These are the bones of my royal father." There's no sadness in her tone, just a solemnity, a quiet acceptance.

"You said he died years ago."

"Yes." A pause, a gathering of thoughts, which Yeva patiently waits out. When Sookhee begins speaking again, it is with a distant voice and gaze, as if she were standing on a high perch looking down at herself. "My family, the royal bloodline, has always had dragon blood. They said we are the descendants of Chuan-pu, and perhaps that's true. But who can really say of a past so distant it's shrouded in fog? My mother had no interest in the touch of men, but with my royal father, when they were both in dragon form—it did not matter, then."

"Your royal father—was he like you? A shape-changer?"

"The opposite, actually. A dragon who sometimes took on human form. He was the last of his kind. Perhaps there are more like him in the remote wilds of this country, or somewhere else entirely—we don't know. There are none that we know of." She grows more pensive. "Like my mother, I have no interest in taking a husband. Since I was little, I'd come to terms with the idea that my family bloodline would end with me."

"So you've said."

She looks sideways at her lover. "Do you want to know how my father died?"

Nothing but the sound of water within the hollow caverns. Yeva nods.

Sookhee's smile grows sad. "I had just turned twelve. I'd come of age and form-changing was new to me, both scary and exciting. I ran wild; I was ungovernable. Against the explicit instructions of my mother I crossed the border of the kingdom. I thought, I am a dragon—why should I care about the laws of mankind? All the folly of youth. I instantly found out that there would always be consequences to breaking such laws. Your guildknights found me, and I was too young, too new to know how to escape their barbs. It was my royal father who saved me, providing another target for their blades while I fled. I survived with nothing more than a few scars"—she gestures to the tangled line seaming her side—"but my royal father was grievously wounded."

Yeva thinks, so what Emory told me was true.

"Your mother came to help us, but his wounds were too great, and he perished. I remember very little from that time, except the grief. The sorrow. My mother never said that she blamed me, but—how could she not? She quarreled with your mother, you know. It was not long after my father died. They were such great friends, and then your mother stopped coming to Quanbao. I'm sure the heartbreak from that period in time sent her to an early grave."

"So all this time my mother knew of your family's secret?"

Sookhee nods.

And Yeva thinks again, if I hadn't left for Mithrandon—if Sookhee's father hadn't died—we might have become friends, naturally introduced. I might have been invited to her court the way my mother was invited. The tragedies of their lives entwine in her mind.

"Yeva, beloved," she says, "when you came I was not sure if the gods were mocking me or sending me a sign. I thought perhaps you were meant to finish the job your compatriots began all those years ago. Or perhaps you were a reminder of the terrible things I had wrought."

"Or perhaps," Yeva says, "I am neither." She's stacking the memories of all her years, one on top of the other: the trauma of her dislocation to Mithrandon, hard metallic days spent training and avoiding the other recruits. Dissolving all the fondness and tenderness she felt for home and family so that it would no longer pain her. Her path to this place, to this moment, has been long and difficult; her trials her own. That she has found comfort in Daqiao is a kindness from the goddess.

Sookhee says: "I had considered letting you take my life, cutting me down with that sacred blade of yours. It seemed suitably poetic to me. Let the girls run the kingdom in my stead. It's what I've trained them for. And they'll have one less secret to hide from the prying eyes of the Empire."

Yeva's shoulders slump. The thought of Varuhelt cutting

through the girl-king's flesh sickens her; she can't bear it. She could never do it. "The Emperor's greed cannot be so easily satisfied," she says. "Your death would be for nothing."

Sookhee leans her head against the edge of Yeva's arm, and she can feel the girl-king's exhaustion in the motion. "But it's too late," she says. "Your captain and his men have already sighted me. They won't leave without a trophy, will they?"

"They will have to." Resolve hardens in her stomach, a protectiveness that she didn't know she was capable of. This crystallization of will brings her clarity, dispelling all doubt, all anxiety. She knows what she can, will, and must do, even in the face of impossible odds.

Sookhee glances at her, eyes shaded with disbelief. She switches to Thrandish, as if to make a point, forcing Yeva to speak in the language that had become second nature to her, against her will. "You'll stand against them, for my sake? If your captain gave you an order to kill me, you would defy him?"

"I would."

Her disbelief remains. "Even if the price was their lives, or mine?"

Vindictiveness swamps her. Maybe if the other guild-knights hadn't been so odious, maybe if they hadn't made her imagine killing them a dozen times on their way to the cavern, maybe then her answer might be different. "I'd do it," she says.

"You'd do what?"

They both turn, startled by this newcomer to their conversation.

Emory stands at the mouth of the hollow, battered but unbowed. Blood pours down half his face, but the musket in his hands glows blue with deadly intent still. He's staring at Yeva, breath ragged. "You'd commit treason, Yeva? You'd do that?"

CHAPTER THIRTEEN

"EMORY." YEVA MOVES toward him, placing her body between him and Lady Sookhee. "Put the weapon away."

His grip on the musket tightens. His gaze yaws wildly between her and the girl-king, and she senses the wheels of his canny mind spinning, dizzy, trying to make the connection between what he's seeing and what he's just experienced. He sees that the massive dragon they were chasing down has vanished, and here is the girl-king, unclothed and trembling, standing upon ground showered with dragon-scale. The rational mind, raised in Mithrandon by books and tools and walls of stone, might come to easier conclusions: that terrible storm dragon somehow swallowed the monarch, and Yeva slayed the beast and cut her out of its belly. But Emory is smarter than that, and Yeva watches him put together the same thing she did.

It's not an answer he can accept. He looks like he's about to tip into madness, about to start foaming at the mouth. He hasn't spent months in Quanbao, slowly being inured to the idea; he hasn't seen the reverence with which Sookhee treated the dragon relics in the mausoleum; he hasn't gone to sleep with Daqiao imprinted behind his eyes and woken up with the taste of the city lingering on his tongue. Emory is a man who lives in a shining white tower and barely ever leaves it. He's never hunted and he's never wielded a weapon with intent to kill. He shakes with nerves as the gun's muzzle wavers between Yeva and the girl-king.

"Put that away," Yeva repeats.

"You'd do it," Emory rasps. He seems so much younger than his age, as if his layers have been peeled back and there stands the boy that Yeva first met in Mithrandon all those years ago. "You'd kill them to protect a beast."

She draws Varuhelt and wakes its blue blade, partly as a threat, but only partly. "I'd do anything to protect her."

"Is your duty so easily cast aside?"

"My duty?" Yeva's grip on her sacred blade tightens. As a guildknight, her path forward should be clear. Her vows to the Sun Emperor are unambiguous: all dragons are a threat. All dragons must be slain. Her maimed right hand is a testimony to the terrible power these creatures hold. She should show no mercy, and hold no regret. If her actions lead to war, to the fall of the kingdom and its sublimation into the Empire, so be it. Such things are beyond her ken and scope of care. She is a tool, doing things that tools must.

Yet, still: Yeva is her mother's daughter. Over the years that connection has frayed to mere threads, but persists, running through her body as strongly as her father's bloodline does, threading through the chambers of her heart. In those newly turned soils are slow-growing saplings of regret, longing, loneliness, love. Emotions she has stopped allowing herself to feel. If she were in Mithrandon, she could easily cut down those tender moods, as has long been her habit. But in the openness of Daqiao, with her armor stripped away and no stone walls to protect her, in this foreign land where she only had herself to hold on to—in this place both alien and familiar, Yeva found herself tending to that garden instead.

She's spent half her life cutting herself into pieces and burying the shards that others considered unsightly. She's walked around as a hollow husk of herself. She's tired of it. She doesn't want to return to Mithrandon and resume her life as usual.

"Yes," she says. "I cast my duty aside. I will not follow the Emperor's orders. I don't care what he wants. I won't do it."

Emory's face twists, and he raises the muzzle of his gun, pointing it at her. It glows, everstone gathering charge.

Yeva's life has always pivoted around the blue fire in her blood, her ability to speak with everstone. It was why she was sent to Mithrandon. It is what she spent years honing. It is what she wields in her course of duty. And the everstone in Emory's musket is everstone like any other, no different from the everstone within Varuhelt. She feels the pulse of its power in the line of her jaw. With casual, practiced ease, she shuts it off.

Emory stares at her in disbelief as his weapon goes dead in his hands. Yeva moves then, striking him in the chest with Varuhelt's hilt, knocking him over. The musket goes clattering to the floor and Yeva kicks it away with one steel-toed boot.

The betrayal that shows in his expression is complete and overwhelming. "How could you?" It comes out sounding childlike. "You'd choose her who you've known for mere months, over those you've known your whole life? Over me, who's been your friend since childhood?"

She stands over him, chest heaving not with exertion but with emotion. What she feels for him is not hatred, but sadness and almost overwhelming pity. Pity, because he seems to be trapped and doesn't know it. "I choose to do the right thing, Emory. I thought you'd understand that too. Why else would you send me here? Why else would you choose the least fit men in the guild to accompany you into Quanbao? Were you not stymying the Emperor's will with your choices?"

Uncertainty flickers on his face. Regret. An understanding that the choices he's made are irreversible. No matter what happens, they can't go back to how they used to be as children. Yeva presses on: "All this time you've said you wanted to be better than your father, to make a kinder, gentler Empire. Is this your idea of what that is?" As Emory takes a sharp breath she continues, relentless. "Is the will of the Emperor more important than I, who've been your friend since childhood?"

Emory turns his face from her, sprawled out on the ground as he is. Tremors shake him. He covers his face. Yeva thinks: he's really not cut out for this sort of work. He should never see battle in a field. But she does not release her grip on Varuhelt. Doesn't let her guard down.

Eventually, he pulls himself back to sitting. "What do you want me to do?" He sounds in despair. "His Radiance expects results, he wants the head of a dragon. You know what his temper is like ... if we return empty-handed, it's not just our heads that will roll. He'll bring his wrath down upon the kingdom ... just as he's always wanted to. He stands in the shadow of his late, great father, the conqueror ... I think he hates that man more than he loves him, you know. His father swept up the neighboring lands and left him with nothing for conquest, nothing to write into the books of legend. . . ."

He's rambling again. "I don't care about that," Yeva says. "What's in His Radiance's heart can stay there. It won't help me, or this situation."

"Enough." Lady Sookhee strides forward, naked yet

unafraid. The skin on her arm is bubbled with damage caused by Emory's weapon, but she seems unaffected by the pain. She points. "If it's a dragon's head you want, then a dragon's head you shall have."

Her finger thrusts toward the skull at the back of the hollow. "Take those bones," she says, "and tell your Emperor you got the job done."

Yeva's eyes widen. "But those bones belonged to your royal father!"

"Yes. And he has no need of them anymore. My father gave up his life for me, many years ago. He would be honored if his remains could once again save me, and the kingdom, even years after his death."

"But your prayers . . ." Yeva thinks of the altar to her own ancestors in her childhood home, the rituals and celebrations that were tied around them. "Are you sure?"

"Prayers are for the living. Not the dead. I am sure, Yeva." She looks down at Emory. "You're a man of letters, a master diplomat. You'll figure out some way to appease the Emperor's appetites with these. Your men—are they alive or dead?"

Emory gets to his feet, slowly. "Mostly alive, I think. We were lucky." He hesitates, steeling himself before he's finally able to face Yeva. "And you, Yeva? Will you return with us?"

He asks, even though it appears he already knows what the answer will be. And as Yeva puts her thoughts into words and her words into breath, all of a sudden her feelings spring into reality, shaping the path of her future. "I will not. I disavow the guild. I put aside my duty. I will not return to Mithrandon."

"And what am I supposed to tell His Radiance, upon my return?"

"Tell him she died," Sookhee says. "Tell him she perished in the hunt for the dragon."

Emory glances between them. "And you—Yeva—you plan to remain here?"

"I'm sure I can find work in the palace," Yeva says. *If they'll have me.* "Barring that, I could still be useful pouring tea."

Sookhee slips a hand into hers. "You'll always have a place by my side."

Emory looks at them both, and you can see understanding crystallize on his face. He looks defeated, wounded. "I tried my best, you know. Yeva, I really tried."

"I know." And she doesn't blame him for what he did. He is the product of his upbringing and circumstance. Born to Empire and tied to it until the day he dies. "But sometimes our best efforts just aren't enough. You'll take care of them for me, won't you? My gryphons. And Sage. They're creatures of the guild. Take them back with you."

CHAPTER FOURTEEN

SO IT IS that the party of guildknights tumbles from the guts of the earth and limps back to Mithrandon, broken but victorious. The company was persuaded, by their guildmaster, to embellish their own roles in the defeat of the dragon, although none were present to witness it, a suggestion taken up with great enthusiasm by the four knights. Captain Joufrey retired with great honor, while the other three rose in esteem within the ranks of the guild. Emory Deerland's report on the affair painted the girl-king of Quentona in such glowing terms, so generous with her hospitality and her aid, that it would seem churlish and petty on the Sun Emperor's part to invent some form of offense as pretext to invasion. In the years to come, Emory Deerland would take it upon himself to negotiate a trade agreement with the kingdom of Quentona, acquiring for the Empire a few ores of precious everstone per year, and His Radiance was swayed into conceding that this state of affairs would be better than engaging in a long and expensive war he can hardly afford.

But that is to come, and in the present moment the masked guildknight is mourned within the walls of Mithrandon. At the same time, the girl-king of Quentona, of Quanbao, gains a new companion, a stranger with a pale and handsome face, said to be a daughter of a close friend of the late king. Not even the Imperial envoys sent years later ever stop to consider that she might be the masked guildknight. So I hear you say, does that mean that the masked guildknight of Mithrandon did not perish in a hunt, but continues to live in Quanbao till this day? And to you I say: that is not true, and the masked guildknight did indeed meet her end down there in that cavern under the earth, never again emerging to face the light of day.

But let us return again to the present. Just over the border between Quanbao and the Empire, a single horse trots up a long, dry path to a village that sits between paddies in fallow, its breath crystallizing in the mouth of the early spring. On its back rides a young woman, wrapped in plain indigo robes, black hair folded into a braid that hangs down her long back. She is unarmed and unadorned, riding up to the cradle of her youth, from which she has been separated for so long. Nostalgia sweeps through her, not like a gentle breeze of recollection, but emotions in tidal waves, breaking over her head and soaking her to the marrow, from which she rises like a goddess, or a newborn child, with eyes that see everything differently. There stand the distant twin peaks she used to watch the sun sink into; there lies the pond full of mudskippers she and her sister used to chase after the rain; and there—there are the familiar roofs of houses, her neighbors' houses, the gray tile of the community hall, and over there—concealed between edifices of white plaster, the shape of her childhood home.

She pulls on the reins and the horse slows. The creature is new to her, a gift from a close friend, and their bond of trust is slowly growing. She has rushed headlong from the capital of Daqiao to this familiar hamlet, but now her resolve stutters, stumbling over its feet in anxiety. For years her return here has been a promise, an abstract thing she could put away as she pleased, tucking it out of sight from her heart. Faced with the chill of the mountain air and weight of the mud on her horse's hooves, she falters. Once she crosses that boundary, once her head passes under the shingled roof that marks the village gate, she will be greeted by the faces of those she left behind so many years ago, and she will see in their eyes what they think of her, so deeply changed by the burdens placed upon her by the Sun Empire.

And yet she has shed those graven stones; in the present moment they no longer press upon her. Her armor she left behind in Quanbao, and her sacred blade she paid a merchant to deliver to Mithrandon. The woman who waits before the gates is only flesh and only blood, one hand curled stiffly around the woven reins of the horse, face bare and chapped by the wind. The molting of that rigid, protective shell has allowed many things to grow in her that have spent years being suppressed. Her chest rushes with questions like a river in spring. There is so much she wants to ask her mother. So much that she needs to learn anew.

None of that will come to her if she stays stiff and still on this thawing path. She knows what she must do. Nudging her heels gently against the horse's flank, she urges it forward.

Yeva is going home.

ACKNOWLEDGMENTS

This manuscript passed through many hands on its way into the world. Thank you to the following people whose insights and wisdom helped shape this book into what it is today: the 2023 Milford Workshop (Jim, Tiffani, Jacey, Janet, Terry, Ida, Chris, Siobhan, Pauline, Akotowaa, Powder, Mariëlle, Liz); the duckies (Avani, George, Sam, Radha, Mike, Adam, Taymour); my agent, DongWon; and my editor, Lindsey, whose patience, wisdom, and trust in my chaotic process is more than I could ever ask for.

ABOUT THE AUTHOR

NEON YANG (THEY/THEM) is the author of four other novellas (*The Red Threads of Fortune, The Black Tides of Heaven, The Descent of Monsters,* and *The Ascent to Godhood*) and one novel (*The Genesis of Misery*). Born and raised in Singapore, they currently live in the UK, where they spend their days avoiding productivity by playing video games. Find them on social media @itsneonyang.